THE COWBOY
and the
GIRL IN THE HOT PINK CHAPS
by
Maggie Carpenter

Published by:

Dark Secrets Press

Ebook Cover Design :

Dark Secrets Press

Visit the author at:

https://www.Amazon.com/author/maggiecarpenter

www.MaggieCarpenter.com

www.facebook.com/MaggieCarpenterWriter[1]

www.twitter.com/magcarpenter2[2]

---

1. http://www.facebook.com/MaggieCarpenterWriter

2. http://www.twitter.com/magcarpenter2

CHAPTER ONE

SLOWLY DRIVING DOWN the main road of the small town, Matt Montgomery noticed three cowgirls lingering outside Annie's Eats, his favorite cafe. Dressed in western show clothes, their competitor's numbers still tied around their waists, they laughed and chatted.

A stream of long, straight, blonde hair suddenly caught his attention.

The girl was tall and lean, but her back was towards him, and the lower half of her body was hidden behind a parked car. Just as he was about to send his eyes back to the road ahead, she and her friends meandered down the sidewalk.

She was wearing hot pink chaps.

"Damn," he muttered under his breath. His border collie, Jinx, let out a whine and gazed up at his master. "You're too young to know, fella."

Jinx whined a second time, but ignoring him, Matt pushed his sunglasses to the top of his head, catching his breath as he followed her slow, ambling walk. The hot pink chaps framed an appealing backside packed into a pair of dark blue jeans. As though sensing his gaze, she turned and looked directly at him.

He darted his eyes back to the road.

The impatient honk of a driver behind him made him jump.

He put his foot down—but risked a second glimpse.

The white T-shirt tucked into her jeans showed off her shapely figure, but a deep frown carved her forehead. Hoping it was curiosity and

1

not anger, he dropped his sunglasses back to the bridge of his nose and continued on.

"Lookin' that good oughta be illegal," he grunted, shaking his head.

Jinx raised his paw and touched his arm.

"Again, you're too young!"

The dog continued to stare at him, then barked twice.

"Okay, fine. Think of a white poodle wearin' a pink, rhinestone collar."

As if understanding, Jinx dropped his paw and began happily panting.

Chuckling as he turned the corner towards his office, Matt turned up the volume on his radio. The topic was the horse show, a six week event nearing the end of its run. The event was a big deal and the community had been bustling.

Riders had trailered in their horses from neighboring counties to compete in everything from team penning to western pleasure. Matthew owned and ran Silver Streak Saddlery, a company started by his father. The overall show champion would win a Silver Streak custom-made saddle.

Growing up in the workroom, he'd fallen in love with the smell of the leather and watching the skilled craftsmen construct the high-end, ornate saddles. Determined to build on his father's success, Matt studied business in college, and followed the latest advances in the developing technology of saddle-fit. His education, talent and passion had transformed Silver Streak Saddlery into a highly respected, national brand. The saddles were listed in the best catalogues, and sold in the finest western tack stores around the country.

Though he'd received offers to branch out into other products, everything from clothing to horse care products, he'd turned them all down. His business was saddle-making, and embarking on a sideline would only be a distraction.

As he rolled into his parking lot, the image of the girl in the hot pink chaps brought a fresh grin to his lips. Jumping from his truck, her image dancing in his mind, he strode into his building with Jinx bounding ahead of him.

"I was getting worried," his secretary declared. "You're late. You're never late."

Jeanette Thompson had been his father's right hand since the company had opened its doors. When the doctors ordered him to stop working and Matt had to takeover the reins, he had begged Jeanette to stay on.

"Sorry, Jeanette, I should've called. I needed that second cup," he remarked, stopping at her desk.

"You also need to settle an argument. Pete and Bob are fighting over who should take the saddle over to the show."

"Since when? Neither of them wanted the job, not that I blame them. Who wants to deal with Sharon? She's a nice enough lady, but a five minute stop turns into an hour, and that's if you're lucky."

Sharon King was the show manager's assistant. Though highly efficient, the woman loved to talk.

"I have no idea what the attraction is," Jeanette replied. "I've asked, but they won't tell me."

"I guess I'd best find out."

"Yes, Matt, you'd better, and soon," she said raising her eyebrows. "They were really going at it a few minutes ago."

"It's an easy argument to settle. I'll take the saddle over myself. I'll just have to suffer through an hour of gardenin' advice, or some other such nonsense. Come on, Jinx, let's see what all the fuss is about."

Walking down the hallway and stopping at the first door, he punched the security code into the high-tech keypad, and slid a card into the slot along the side. There was a beep, a green light blinked, and he pushed it open.

When it came to security, Matt spared no expense. Tens of thousands of dollars in saddles and raw materials sat in the workroom. Walking into the large space with Jinx trotting ahead, the door swung shut behind him. Peering around the expansive room, he spotted his two best salesmen standing by the coffee machine.

Striding forward he waved his greetings to the various workers who were cutting the leather, punching out personalized silver ornamentation, and crafting the saddles. He loved the sounds and smells. Knowing how much his father missed it, Matt made it a point to bring him in at least twice a week.

"I understand you two have a debate goin' on," he said as he approached.

Matt was only slightly older, but his deep knowledge of the business and his natural authority had earned their respect. Even the grizzled craftsmen who had worked side-by-side with his father in the early days held Matt in high-regard. He saw the company as one big family, and while he knew there would always be spats, he did his best to shut them down quickly with as little drama as possible. Pete and Bob were naturally competitive, but they enjoyed a camaraderie, and Matt wanted to shut down any discord before it became something more.

"You wanna tell me what the problem is?"

"Not really," Pete muttered.

"I will," Bob said, thrusting his hands in his pockets. "We've been to tryin' decide who should take the saddle over to the show office. I suggested a coin toss, but—"

"Hold on," Matt interrupted. "Last I heard, neither of you wanted to go over there. What's changed?"

The two men exchanged a look.

"Is this about a girl?"

"Yeah, I guess you could say that," Bob replied. "Her name is Dusty somethin', and she's been cleanin' up in the barrel racin' events."

"Okay," Matt said slowly, completely mystified by their quarrel, "and why does that have anything to do with deliverin' the saddle?"

"She has everyone talkin'," Pete declared. "She rides a black geldin' who's supposedly as fast as a bullet train."

"You've both seen plenty of fast horses. Come on, the whole story."

"She wears hot pink chaps and—"

"Hot pink chaps?" Matt repeated, not meaning to cut him off.

"Yeah, can you believe it? She wears hot pink chaps and has blonde hair almost to her ass, and she's supposedly hot, like, really hot. I'm dyin' to see her ride. Hell, I'm just dyin' to see her, period."

"Yeah, well you're not the only one," Bob chimed in. "You've got a girlfriend. I'm the single guy around here."

"I'll ask again," Matt said, trying to stay patient, "what does this have to do with deliverin' the saddle?"

"We've heard she's good friends with Sharon and helps around the office," Pete said. "We figured she'll probably be there at some point."

"Finally!" Matt exclaimed. "We'll all go, and if she's there we can salivate together. I'm gonna pick up dad, then we can load the saddle into my truck and caravan it over there."

"Damn, Matt, that's why I like workin' for you," Pete said with a chuckle. "You always have the answers."

"If she's that good lookin' and that sexy, she'll be taken anyway," Matt reasoned, "and speakin' of goin' to the show, how many saddles have you sold since it started? A dozen or more?"

"About," Pete nodded.

"Let's end with a bang. Whoever brings in the most sales by the end of the week will get a bonus."

"What kinda bonus?" Pete asked.

"An extra 5% on every saddle sold."

"Blow my whistle," Bob exclaimed. "That's a deal."

"Just do me a favor and don't kill each other," Matt pleaded with a grin. "Come on, Jinx, up to the office. I've got some work to do before we can leave."

Jinx bounded towards the staircase that led up to Matt's office, and as Matt followed him, he flashed back to the beautiful blond he'd seen on the street. She had to be the girl the boys were fighting over, and they were right. She was as hot as a tin roof in the middle of summer.

"The way she looked at me, though," he muttered, "that was weird."

AS MATT WAS SETTLING down to work, Dusty Anderson was walking into the show office, though it was actually just temporary trailer brought in for the event. Dusty was delivering a cappuccino to Sharon King. Sharon was her aunt.

"Thanks, Dot," Sharon said gratefully. "It sure is good having you out of college. I know you didn't go far, but it felt like you did. I never got to see you."

"I missed you too, Aunt Sharon, but can you please call me Dusty. Dot isn't who I am anymore."

"Dusty," she said with a resigned sigh. "If that's what you want."

"It is. I leave my competition in the dust! That's part of why I chose it."

"You're not going to tell me the other part?"

"Maybe one day."

"What's the matter? You don't look so happy. Are you worried about the race this afternoon?"

"Not at all. Licorice and I will win," she said confidently, "and it doesn't matter even if I don't. I'll still be the division champion and eligible for the national finals."

"That is so exciting, but I can see something has upset you. What happened, honey?"

"I saw someone," she mumbled. "Someone I used to know."

"A boy?"

"He's not a boy anymore. We've both grown up."

"You'll always be a little girl to me," Sharon said softly, "but this, uh, man, tell me about him."

"Nothing much to tell. It was a lifetime ago."

"But you still have feelings for him?"

"I'll always have feelings for him, but he doesn't even remember who I am."

"How do you know that?"

"He drove past me and we shared a look. It was obvious he had no clue."

"I'm guessing he'll figure it out, and when he does and gets in touch, I'll be right here if you need to talk."

"Thanks, but I'm not so sure. Why would he? It was a fleeting moment, that's all."

"Funny thing about those moments," Sharon remarked thoughtfully. "You bend down to tie your shoe, you look the other way, stop to grab an extra cup of coffee, and those few seconds don't happen."

"What's your point?"

"The moment happened. That's fate. You'll be seeing him again, you mark my words."

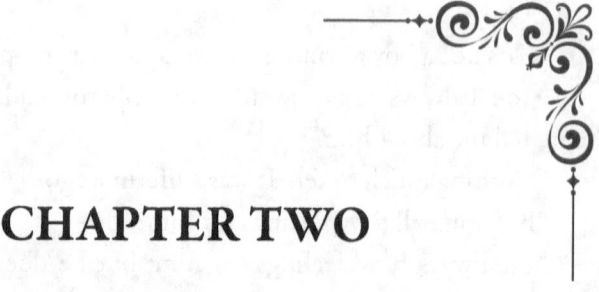

CHAPTER TWO

LEAVING HER AUNT'S office, Dusty was marching back to her horse's barn when she spotted Matt's silver truck roll to a stop outside the trailer. Quickly slipping behind a food van, she watched him step from the cab, then unload a saddle wrapped in a protective cover. Moments later, Jinx jumped out and began busily sniffing at the ground.

"Oh, Jinxy," she muttered, her heart melting as she watched the dog. "I haven't seen you in ages."

But to her chagrin, he paused, lifted his nose to the air and looked in her direction.

"Uh-oh. No, Jinxy, don't come over here."

She'd known the border collie since he was a puppy. In days past, when she'd run into Matt in town with Jinx at his side, she'd find the courage to ask if she could pet his adorable canine. Not only did she adore Jinx, petting him was the perfect excuse to talk to the handsome cowboy. If he had an attractive girl on his arm, she'd swallow her jealousy and act like she didn't care.

But now Jinx was trotting towards her.

The last thing she wanted was for Matt to see her lurking.

She darted her eyes towards the trailer.

He was halfway up the steps.

"Jinx, let's go," he called, looking across at his dog. "Come on, boy."

To her great relief, Jinx turned and trotted off.

For a split second she considered going back to see her aunt, but even if she found the courage she didn't have enough time—and she wasn't even sure she wanted to risk seeing him. He hadn't recognized her on the street, and if he didn't remember her up close and personal she'd feel like crap.

"But why should he?" she muttered. "It's been too long. I was a nobody and he was a somebody. Now he's an even bigger somebody. No, I'm not going to make a fool of myself, especially not before my class."

But as he and Jinx disappeared inside the trailer, she stood, staring, wishing she could snap her fingers and make him magically appear before her. Letting out a sigh, her mind flashed to her favorite fantasy.

Their first kiss.

He'd clutch the back of her hair and mumble how desperately he wanted her, then devour her lips and make her weak at the knees.

"Oh, Matt, how long am I going to carry these feelings?" she whispered with a heavy sigh. "It's pointless. Even if you did notice me, it would never go anywhere. I'm sure you've got girls lined up at your door."

Trying to push away the pangs in her heart, she turned to walk away, but noticed a couple of SUV's pulling to a stop behind Matt's truck. Pausing, she watched two well-dressed cowboys climb out, trot up the stairs and enter the trailer. In spite of her frustration she had to grin. She could easily imagine the testosterone flying around her aunt's office.

"You can handle them, Auntie," she muttered with a giggle, then turned and continued on her way to see Licorice, her coal-black gelding.

Stabling him at the show wasn't her first choice, but she couldn't afford the cost of transporting him back and forth from her parents small ranch. She'd been grateful when the show's schedule came out and she'd found her events were listed on consecutive days. Showing was expensive, and she couldn't afford paying for board on days she wasn't in a class.

"Are you ready, Dusty?"

Deep in thought, she jumped and spun around. Patrick O'Neal, her trainer and boss, was striding towards her. The man was an anomaly. He was gay, Irish, and a former show jumper who had unexpectedly traded in his crash helmet for a cowboy hat. At the beginning of the summer, just as the show season was starting, his assistant had unexpectedly quit. To her surprise and great joy, he'd offered Dusty the position. Not only would she have a stipend and free training, Patrick's belief in her had done wonders for her confidence. Now she was ending the year the winner of her division.

"I'm so ready," she replied, jogging up to him. "I can't wait to get out there."

"I know you already have the division title in the bag, but don't slack off now. You want to end with a win. How are you feeling?"

"Great. You know the only real competition is Trixie Davenport, but I'll beat her. I'll vibe her out."

"I think those hot pink chaps vibed out all your challengers," he said with a wink, "and Licorice probably gallops as fast as he does because he thinks a pink monster is chasing him."

"Patrick, stop," she said, laughing out loud, "that's not true. Licorice is fast because Licorice is fast."

The first paycheck she'd received from Patrick had been spent on the unique chaps. It had been an impetuous purchase, something she'd done on a whim. When she'd returned home, put them on and stared at her reflection, she'd wondered if she'd ever be brave enough to actually wear them. It was just a couple of weeks later that her worn-out, brown suede chaps fell apart. Unable to buy another pair, she'd had no choice.

Once in the saddle, she'd discovered they were exceptionally comfortable, almost like a second skin. With no alternative she had to use them at the horse shows, and something surprising happened. The cowboys began to notice her. Boys had never paid her any attention, and the unexpected flirting lifted her spirits and contributed further to her self-assurance.

She'd been an awkward teenager. Tall, skinny, braces on her teeth, short, mousey brown hair, and almost blind without her thick, coke-bottle glasses.

The barn had been her sanctuary.

The horses didn't care about her appearance, or that she was ungainly and shy. They only cared that she doted on them, brought them treats, and happily, endlessly, rubbed their necks and scratched their ears. They'd nicker when she walked down the barn aisle, trot up to her when she entered their paddocks, and there was no question she was going to make horses her future profession.

Before she started college the braces came off, and in her junior year she underwent laser eye surgery. With her teeth stunningly perfect, no glasses perched on her nose, and her figure suddenly blooming, she decided it was time to address the hair she'd always hated. Using over-the-counter hair lighteners, the mousey color changed to honey blonde, and she let it grow. Almost overnight she was staring at a stranger in the mirror, and found herself facing life with a growing confidence and poise.

Now striding back to the barn with Patrick, she pulled her mind away from Matt, and focused on the event ahead.

"Please tell me the groom remembered to put the pink polos on Licorice, and not the white ones."

"He knows," Patrick assured her. "After the way you told him off last time he wouldn't dare forget."

The bandages wrapped around the horse's legs for protection were available in a rainbow of colors, and Dusty had switched from white to pink for the end of season show.

"Told him off?" she said with a giggle. "I love your Irish expressions, Patrick."

"You can take the boy out of Ireland, but you can't take Irish out of the boy."

"Apparently!"

"Jump on and I'll meet you in the warm-up ring."

They had reached the barn, but she couldn't resist one last look across the grounds at the trailer. The trucks were still parked outside. It was odd. Almost six weeks had passed and she hadn't seen Matt once, and he'd shown up just when she was about to ride in her most important class. Patrick was right. She needed to go to the nationals with a win under her belt. Turning away and entering the barn, she walked up to Licorice waiting patiently in the cross ties. Lovingly stroking his neck, she gazed into his deep brown eyes.

"We're going to blow everyone out of the water today," she said softly. "Anyone who's watching is going to drop their jaw. Right big fella?"

As her horse snorted and brushed his head against her, she sank against his neck.

"Patrick calls us Lickety Split, and that's what we have to be today."

Feeding him a treat from her pocket, then moving to his side, she spotted the back of Trixie Davenport a short distance away. Trixie was her nemesis. The girl came from a wealthy family and owned several horses, each of them worth a great deal of money.

Dusty had found Licorice wasting away in a backyard. Though he'd been in terrible condition, her sharp eye had seen his perfect confirmation. When a motorbike had zoomed by and spooked him, he'd taken off like a rocket, then trotted up to the fence where she'd been standing.

It had been love at first sight.

She'd persuaded her parents to let her knock on the door of the house and see if he was for sale. Two days later, she and Patrick had driven up and hauled him away.

Though she had Patrick's support, she had been responsible for his rehabilitation. With very little money it hadn't been easy, but she'd found him secondhand blankets for the winter, and searched out the best supplements. As the weeks passed her care began to show, and the transformation was remarkable. She'd thought he might have potential, but it never occurred to her, or anyone else, the horse would possess such remarkable athletic ability.

Standing beside him and staring across at Trixie, Dusty grimaced. She didn't think much of her competitor's riding ability, but Trixie had an outstanding gelding called Harrison Hare. Moving quietly across the barn aisle, Dusty stood behind the tack room door, placing herself just a few feet from her rival, but out of sight. Tilting her head to the side, Dusty decided she had nothing to worry about.

"Your position's all wrong around the second barrel," she murmured, watching Trixie lift her expensive phone from her jacket pocket. "That's why you lose precious time."

With a knowing grin, Dusty walked into the tack room and picked up her saddle.

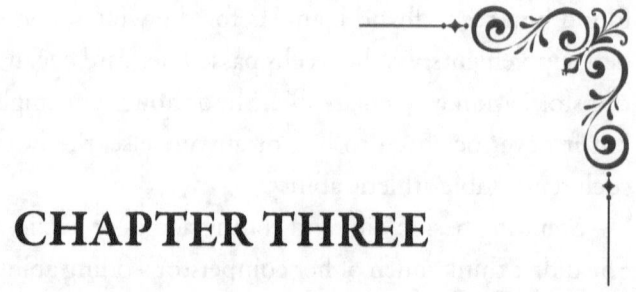

CHAPTER THREE

DUSTY HAD BEEN STUNNED at the speed and agility Licorice had shown when she'd started his training. He was so talented she often wondered how he'd ended up wasting away in a backyard. Now waiting in the short tunnel leading into the arena, he couldn't stand still.

Just as fired up and eager to race, the adrenalin pumped through Dusty's veins. She loved the few seconds before they bolted forward. Every nerve in her body sparked. Waiting for the cue, she reminded herself not to push. If she left her horse alone to do his job it would result in a top performance.

The call came.

She let him loose.

Bolting forward, he burst into the arena.

Flying around the first barrel he charged to the second, but cut it so close she had a fleeting moment of panic. Coming out of the super-sharp turn he surged to the last, and when he curled his body around it and exploded for home, she knew they had clocked an incredibly fast time. As they slowed down in the exit tunnel, the cheering of the crowd reached her ears.

"Unbelievable," Patrick declared running up to meet her and grabbing the reins. "Absolutely unbelievable."

Jumping from the saddle and raising her fist in the air as she let out a triumphant cry, then threw her arms around her horse's neck.

"You're brilliant, big boy. You're absolutely brilliant!"

"You were amazing," Patrick exclaimed. "Trixie's up soon. I doubt she'll beat the time you just clocked."

"Are she and Bill here yet?" she asked breathlessly. "I hope they are. I hope they saw that."

Bill was Trixie's trainer. He'd be ticked off, and she hoped her super-fast time would have unnerved her opponent.

"They must be lurking around somewhere," Patrick replied with a grin.

"I'd love to see their faces right now. I have a feeling Trixie's going to try just a bit too hard."

"Dusty," he said, dropping his voice and giving her a knowing look. "What have you done?"

"I haven't done anything," she said innocently. "Why would you say that?"

"I told you what we did to wicked girls back in Ireland who pulled dirty tricks. We'd swat their bottoms. The last time you pulled a stunt I warned you that's exactly what would happen if you did it again, and I meant it."

"Patrick," she groaned rolling her eyes.

"I'm serious. I know how competitive you are, and how badly you want to win."

"I'll win because I have the best horse and I'm the best rider," she interrupted. "Now I'm going to walk him, but I'll be back in time to see Trixie's run."

"I don't think you have to worry about her beating you," he remarked, wondering if he'd mistaken the mischievous look in her eye.

"I'm not worried, not a bit."

Watching from the sidelines, Matt and his two salesmen had been spellbound. Not only had the speed of her horse been jaw-dropping, the pink polo wraps around his black legs, Dusty's hot pink chaps, and her blonde hair flying out from under her black cowboy hat, had been a captivating scene.

"That was a helluva ride," Pete mumbled. "What did you think, Matt?"

"I think that's about as good as it gets," he declared. "Who was that competitor? Dusty what?"

"I think they said Anderson," Bob replied.

"Huh, Dusty Anderson. That name rings a vague bell. Anderson. Common enough I expect. Well, Jinx, I guess we'd better be gettin' back to the office."

"You're not gonna stay and see who wins?" Bob asked.

"I think that's a given. How many more are there?"

"Just a handful. It's only a few minutes."

"Now that I think about it, maybe I should offer to award the prize."

"Do it," Bob said enthusiastically. "It'll give us an excuse to meet her."

"Yeah, for sure, do it," Pete said eagerly.

"How can I say no?" Matt said with grin. "Come on, Jinx, let's go see the ring manager."

"Wait. Trixie Davenport's up next," Bob said urgently. "If anyone can beat Miss Hot Pink Chaps, it's her."

"Davenport, as in, Davenport Steel?"

"Yep, that's the one. She has real expensive horses. I sold her a saddle here last week."

"Huh. Okay. Let's see how she does."

Moment's later Trixie Davenport erupted into the ring. Though she looked quick rounding the first barrel, when she started around the second she leaned perilously sideways. As she sped off to the third it was obvious she'd lost valuable seconds, and when her time was posted she'd landed in fourth place.

In the rear of the starting tunnel, Patrick noticed Dusty had returned without Licorice and was loitering in the shadows behind Trixie's trainer. As Trixie breathlessly dropped from her horse and handed the reins to a groom, she put her hands on her hips, stared at the ground and kicked the dirt. Patrick could almost hear her silent cursing.

"What were you doin' with your body?" Bill demanded. "You were leanin' so far over that second barrel you could've got him off balance."

"Trying to make my time faster."

"Who told you to do that?"

"Uh, no-one."

Glancing across at Dusty and seeing her slink away, Patrick quickly started off after her.

"Hey, Dusty, are you ready to collect your prize?" Patrick asked catching up.

"Hi, Patrick. I'm absolutely thrilled. I'm just off to get Licorice."

"Anything you want to tell me?"

"Like what?"

"Like, would you have any idea why Trixie was leaning so badly around that second barrel?"

"Why would I?"

"One of these days..."

"One of these days, what?"

"You'll get your comeuppance."

"What do you mean by that?"

"You and I are going to have a serious talk before you leave today. Hurry up and get Licorice. You have to go in."

A short time later, the crowd cheering, she jogged in with her gleaming black gelding trotting along next to her, but her heart suddenly skipped, and her beaming smile froze.

Matt was standing in the ring waiting to present her prize.

WATCHING THE SPARKLING young woman slow to a walk as she approached, Matt felt a strange rolling in his stomach. She looked familiar, but he couldn't imagine forgetting such a beauty.

"Great ride, Dusty," the ring manager declared. "Let's get a photo of you accepting your trophy, and the check from Mr. Montgomery."

"Yes, sure."

"Matt, this is Dusty Anderson," the manager said with a wide smile. "Dusty, this is Matthew Montgomery from Silver Streak Saddlery. As you know he's one of our sponsors."

"Great to meet you," Matt said warmly, extending his hand. "That was a great ride. I've never seen it done better."

"Thanks. It was a great ride because I've got a great horse," she replied. "That's the thing about horses. They're honest and loyal. Did you know they have incredible memories? They never forget a friend. Never."

"Uh, right," he nodded, unable to read her odd expression. "Anyway, uh, here's your trophy and check. Congratulations."

A photographer stepped forward, snapped some pictures, and the small group began to break up, but Pete and Bob had been taking care of Jinx and watching from the tunnel. It was a golden opportunity to meet the girl in the hot pink chaps and they weren't about to let it slip through their fingers. Jogging into the arena, Jinx raced ahead of them, but he didn't run to Matt. He made a beeline for Dusty.

"Wow, he really likes you," Matt remarked as his border collie began whining and jumping on her.

"I'll walk Licorice back to the barn," Patrick offered, stepping up and taking the reins.

"Thanks, Patrick," she said gratefully, thrilled to be petting Jinx again.

Crouching down and making a fuss of the happy canine, the dog jumped all over her and kissed her face, overjoyed to see his old friend.

"If I didn't know better I'd swear he knows you," Matt declared. "He doesn't take to strangers like that. I've never seen him act this way before."

"He's a wonderful dog, aren't you, Jinxy."

A frown crept across Matt's face. A while back someone else used to call him Jinxy.

"Hey, I really enjoyed your ride," Pete said, stepping up.

"Yeah, me too," Bob added. "Fantastic."

"Thanks, well, time for me to go. Nice to meet you, Mr. Montgomery," she said formally as she straightened up, then abruptly turning, she strode towards the gate.

GRIPPING HER TROPHY and check, frustrated tears brimmed in her eyes. Unable to stand it another minute, she hurried past the show staff and into the ladies room.

"Dammit," she hissed, leaning against the wall. "This is a nightmare."

"What do you have to complain about?"

Darting her eyes up, she saw Trixie Davenport standing by the wash basins.

"What you did wasn't cool," the dark-haired girl spat.

"Hey, if you don't know how to ride you've only got yourself to blame," Dusty snapped. "All you know how to do is sit on an expensive horse, hang on, and kick the shit out of it to make it go faster. How would you like someone wailing into your ribs? You're a horrible rider. The only animal you should be allowed to sit on is a pack mule."

"Jeez, what's wrong with you?" Trixie said, staring at her. "Take a chill pill."

As her rival moved quickly past her and out the door, Dusty moved across to the wash basin. Staring into the mirror she recalled the many times she'd given Jinx treats and made a fuss of him. Though she knew her appearance had changed, it hurt like hell that Matt had no idea who she was.

"My wonderful horse and my riding, that's all I should be thinking about," she muttered, determined to get the handsome cowboy out of her head. "I'm done with this crap. Screw him. I'm going to see Licorice, then show Aunt Sharon my trophy. It's time to forget about fucking Matthew Montgomery!"

Taking a deep breath, she opened the door, and keeping her eyes to the ground, she moved through the crowd towards the exit.

"Dusty?"

Her heart jumped.

She paused her step and raised her eyes.

"Hi," Matt said with a grin. "I wondered if you'd like to have some coffee sometime, or maybe lunch."

"You can't be serious?" she quipped, unable to stop the words spilling from her lips.

"Uh, have I offended you?"

"Offended me? You're asking if you've offended me?"

"Easy there," he said lifting his palm in a gesture of surrender as he slowly moved towards her. "If I have, please tell me. Let me make it up to you."

An angry bubble suddenly formed in her gut and began moving slowly upwards. The exasperated years she'd spent adoring him, all the while knowing she'd been nothing but an ugly duckling not worthy of his attention, suddenly exploded in a torrent of emotion.

"I wouldn't have coffee with you if you were the last man on the planet," she shouted, glaring at him with contempt blazing from her eyes. "You don't know me, but you like the long blonde hair, perfect teeth and the hot pink chaps. That's what you want—not me! Go and find some dingbat like Trixie Davenport. I'm sure she'd love to be seen with the famous Matt Montgomery."

Out of breath, out of words, and completely infuriated, she made a loud, irritated grunting noise, then hurried away, but not letting his long lost friend leave without a goodbye, Jinx bounded after her.

Though completely confused, and not sure if he should give chase, Matt had no choice. He had to run after Jinx. Catching up with his dog outside the arena, Dusty was only a short distance ahead.

"Hey, Dusty, wait a second."

"What?" she snapped, spinning around to face him.

"I don't know what I've done to upset you, but that temper tantrum—"

"Temper tantrum?" she barked, cutting him off. "How dare you! Just because you're a good looking guy with a fancy truck and money to burn, you think I should be all google-eyed."

"Google-Eyed? Dammit, what the heck are you goin' on about?"

Upset by the argument Jinx began to bark. Bending down to reassure him, Dusty laid her trophy on the grass.

"Jinxy, don't worry sweetie," she said affectionately. "You just have an idiot human for an owner."

"What the hell have I done?" Matt demanded. "What's wrong with you?"

"Oh, so now there's something wrong with me!" she shrilled, jumping to her feet. "There's not a damn thing wrong with me. I only go out with someone because they're genuinely interested in me. A guy who wants to spend time with me because of who I am, not how I look."

They were suddenly leaning towards each other, eye to eye, two wild beasts in a standoff.

"You know what you need?" he said, lowering his voice as a deep furrow carved his forehead. "An old-fashioned spankin'."

"What did you just say?"

"You heard me. You're upset about somethin', okay, but damn, girl, the least you can do is tell me what it is. That was nothin' but a childish outburst."

"You know what," she hissed, knowing in one more second she'd dissolve into tears, "maybe you're right, maybe that was a tantrum, and maybe I do need a spanking, but it sure as hell won't come from the likes of you."

Dumbfounded, he watched her grab her trophy and storm off. Realizing there was no point going after her, he shook his head and looked down at his dog.

"Don't even think about doin' that again! Chase rabbits, not girls."

But as Jinx whined his reply, Matt spied an envelope lying on the ground. Picking it up, he discovered it was Dusty's check.

"Whatta ya think, Jinx? Should we take this over to the office, or maybe deliver it ourselves? I think maybe we'll find out where Patrick O'Neal keeps horses stabled and wander on over there."

CHAPTER FOUR

PATRICK HAD A SURPRISE waiting for Dusty's return. He'd arranged a party to celebrate her victory. A few of his younger students had dashed to the food truck to buy some drinks and cakes, then set them up on tack trunks in the barn aisle.

Taking the stiff white card that had been Dusty's competition number, he'd flipped it over and written SURPRISE with a black felt tip pen across the back, and taped it to the wall outside the tack room. Besides the trophy and check, Dusty had also received a blanket for Licorice. The groom had cleaned him up and draped it over the horse's back.

"Where is she?" one of the young students complained. "She should be back by now."

"She'll be here," Patrick assured her. "She doesn't know Licorice has been groomed and she'll want to do that before she does anything else, trust me."

When he saw her enter the barn at the far end and march towards them, he knew something was wrong. He'd been her friend and mentor since she was a self-conscious and insecure adolescent. Though she was now a self-confident and beautiful young woman, certain characteristics hadn't changed. One of those was her walk. When she was upset she would take long, determined strides.

"Something's wrong," the girl mumbled. "She only takes big steps like that when she's mad."

"I'd say that's a good bet," Patrick agreed. "I'll go and see what's up."

Though Dusty could see the small gathering ahead, she was still upset after her fight with Matt. The last thing she wanted was to chat with the excited young girls. Then Patrick started towards her. He could read her like a book. There would be no escaping his questions.

"What's wrong?" he asked as he approached. "Everyone is thrilled with your win and they want to celebrate with you. They've prepared a little party."

"They have?" she mumbled, feeling guilty for not wanting to join them. "That's so thoughtful."

"You know how they look up to you. Whatever's upset you, can you put it aside for a few minutes?"

Letting out a sigh, and pushing Matt to the back of her mind, she nodded her head.

"I will, yes, for them. It's very sweet, of course I can."

"We can talk later if you want," Patrick offered, putting his arm around her shoulders.

"There's nothing to talk about. Let's get this party started."

Forcing a smile, she hurried down the aisle to the excited gang waiting to greet her.

"You were awesome," one of the young girls yelled as she reached them.

"Thanks, Amanda. Why don't you put this trophy in the tack room for me while I give my amazing boy a big carrot? He did all the work. He deserves all the attention!"

"I can take your trophy? Really?" the youngster beamed. "Yes, please."

Dusty handed her the large, silver cup, then grabbing some carrots, with the gaggle of girls following her, she walked across to her horse.

Patrick knew something very disturbing had happened, but he still intended to have a talk with her before the day was done. He was determined to uncover what had transpired with Trixie Davenport.

MATT HAD DECIDED TO wait until later in the day to find Dusty and return her check. He wanted to give her time to cool down, and he needed to settle as well, but he also wanted to figure out what he'd done or said to make her so angry. Jumping into his truck he headed back into town.

"I think we should stop for some coffee and a bite to eat. Whatta ya say, Jinx?"

Jinx barked his agreement, and a short time later Matt was seated at his favorite table on the outside patio of Annie's Eats. The cafe was his second home.

"Hey, Matt, what can I get you?"

The waitress, Mary Jo, was the daughter of the owner, and had worked there every summer for as long as Matt could remember.

"Burger, fries, coffee," he smiled, "but the coffee first. How's college?"

"It's always nice to come home, but I love it."

"When do you go back?"

"In a couple of weeks. I miss it, but then I miss this place when I'm there. It's weird."

"That sounds pretty normal. I was the same. It's excitin' and fun to be away, but there's no bed like your own, and nothin' like bein' around your family."

"Would Jinx like some water?" she asked, reaching down to pat him.

"He would, thanks."

As she ambled away, Matt leaned back and thought about Dusty Anderson's diatribe. She had yelled at him as if they'd known each other for years, and Jinx had been thrilled to see her.

"Jinxy," he muttered. "I definitely remember someone calling you by that name. Who the hell was it?"

"He's such a cutie," Mary Jo said, placing the dog's water on the ground, "and here's your coffee, Matt."

"Thanks," Matt replied, immediately picking it up from the table and taking a drink. "Mary Jo, before you leave I've gotta question for you. Can you remember anyone who used to call Jinx, Jinxy?"

"I don't think so, but I'm not sure I'd remember something like that."

"What about the name Dusty Anderson? Does that ring a bell? A cowgirl. She owns a horse called Licorice?"

"Huh. Well, I don't ride, so I don't really know that crowd, but there was a Dot Anderson who used to come here a lot. I haven't seen her in ages. Matt? Matt, are you okay."

"It can't be," he muttered under his breath.

"Matt?"

"Sorry," he said quickly. "You just answered my question. It's hard to believe."

"I'll be back in a minute."

But he barely heard her.

The sexy, gorgeous girl calling herself Dusty, was Dot Anderson, the skinny, timid church mouse with braces and coke bottle glasses who used to hang around outside the cafe. He wasn't that much older, but she'd been so shy and awkward he'd tried to befriend her through Jinx.

"Why didn't she just tell me?" he muttered. "At least the mystery's solved and I can straighten this out, but damn, what a temper, and how the hell could she expect me to recognize her? She looks completely different, and I haven't seen her for, what, four, five years? I was right, she does need someone to paddle that gorgeous butt of hers. Talk about throwin' a hissy fit."

BACK AT THE BARN, THE party was over and the girls had gone their separate ways. Sitting in the tack room, Dusty idly flipped through a horse magazine waiting for the trailer to arrive. She had no more classes, and Licorice was going home.

"Hello there," Patrick said as he ambled in. "Are you waiting for Jeb?"

"Yep. He just called. He won't be long."

"You're more than welcome to keep Licorice at my barn. He won't be in a stall. We have those two empty paddocks out back."

"Thanks, Patrick, but I like him at home."

"It will save you all that time riding him back and forth."

"But we get there warmed up, then we enjoy the relaxing trail ride home."

"Just know the offer stands if you need it. Now on to other matters. Do you want to tell me what got you so upset earlier?"

"Nope, but I'm worried about my check. I can't find it anywhere."

"You lost your check? How?"

"If I knew how, I'd know where to look," she replied briskly, though she hadn't meant to snap at him.

"There's no need to be snippy. Your aunt can cancel it and issue a new one tomorrow if she has to."

"Sorry. I'm just tired, and I know she can, that's why I'm not totally freaking out."

"Dusty, we need to have a talk," he said solemnly, perching on a tack trunk opposite her.

"This sounds serious. Should I be worried?"

"It is serious, and maybe you should," he replied, fixing her with a steady gaze. "You're not going anywhere until you tell me what happened with Trixie. What did you say to her that made her almost topple off her horse?"

"She was never going to fall out of her saddle. That thing she rides in is an armchair."

"That wasn't an answer."

"I didn't say anything to her, and that's the truth."

"I know you, and I saw that look in your eye. I also saw you shadowing her after her bad performance. Dusty, I know you did something. Spit it out."

"Fine," she said sighing dramatically. "I *may* have had a conversation with, uh, let's say, an imaginary friend, and Trixie *may* have been in earshot, and I *may* have said something about her saving precious seconds if she leaned to the side going around the second barrel."

The speed with which Patrick bolted off his tack trunk and yanked her to her feet stunned her, but the ease with which he quickly bent her over and wrapped an arm around her waist shocked her even more.

"Patrick, what the hell are you doing?"

"I warned you if you pulled any more stunts I'd spank you," he said sharply, "and that's exactly what I'm going to do!"

"Don't you dare!"

Ignoring her protest he dispatched a series of strong swats crisscrossing her backside, then rained his hand on the delicate area where her thighs meet her cheeks.

"Patrick! Ow! Ow! Please stop!"

"This lesson needs to be brought home," he scolded sharply. "I told you what I'd do if you attempted any more of your sneaky, cunning schemes."

"Okay! Stop! Okay!"

His hand carried a hot sting, but her deep embarrassment hurt more.

"Now," he said sternly standing her up and gripping her arms, "I'm only going to say this one time. Are you paying attention?"

"Yes," she mewled, afraid to raise her eyes to his, knowing her face was probably as red as her backside.

She'd known Patrick for over a decade. He'd been like a second brother, and she considered him her best friend. She hadn't thought, even for a minute, he'd carry out his threat.

"Look at me."

Tentatively lifting her gaze, she searched his eyes for some understanding, but to her dismay she saw only steely determination.

"This conniving streak of yours stops today. You're going to the national finals, and you absolutely cannot pull any of your foolish crap there. If you do, and you're caught, you'll not only ruin your reputation, mine will suffer right along with it. Most of the competitors at that level will be sharp, and if they so much as sniff something, your ass will be hauled before the judging committee faster than you rode Licorice today. Am I clear?"

"Uh-huh."

"I just whacked your ass for both our sakes. You will not gamble with your future, and you sure as hell won't gamble with mine. If anything like this ever happens again, you're out of the barn."

"Patrick! You can't mean that."

"I'm afraid I do. You've grown into a gorgeous young woman, but sometimes you still act like a bratty teenager. It's time to get your act together. Don't you understand, Dusty? You're entering the big league. You know I love you, and I might spank you again if it's warranted, but not for this. There's no second chance with this. Cheating won't fly. Understood?"

"I understand, and I'm sorry," she bleated. "I promise I'll be clean as a whistle from now on."

Uncurling his fingers from around her upper arms, he pulled her against his chest and hugged her.

"If I wasn't batting for the other team I'd be hard pressed not to want you for myself."

"I wish you weren't," she whimpered. "You didn't care how I looked when I came wandering into your barn all those years ago. You didn't care how clumsy I was or how scared I was. You made me feel like I belonged. You cared about who I was, not how I looked, and...and..."

The emotional drama of the day swept over her, and breaking into heavy sobs she buried her head in his chest.

"Hey, why are you crying? I didn't spank you that hard—though I was tempted," he joked, trying to make her smile.

"I just wish..."

"What? You just wish what?"

"Other men were like you, except, you know, straight."

Finally breaking away, she wiped her eyes and stared up at him.

"Sorry."

"There's no need to apologize."

"It's been a really weird day," she sniffled, wiping her face. "Weird, and, uh, great, and very confusing."

"Do you want to talk about it?"

"Not really."

"Are you going to celebrate tonight?"

"Aunt Sharon and mom are taking me out for dinner."

"Good. Let your hair down. Have one drink too many."

"I'm going to have more than one," she quipped, thinking she'd like nothing better than to get buzzed.

"Do you want me to wait with you until the trailer gets here?"

"No, I think I'm going to hang out with Licorice."

"You do that."

"Okay. Thanks, Patrick, and you don't have to worry. I got the message."

"I certainly hope so," he said kissing her forehead. "Call me if you need me, and take the day off tomorrow. You've earned it. We only have a couple of classes and I have plenty of help."

"Thanks. That would be great. I need to sleep in."

Giving her a last quick hug, he picked up his satchel and headed out. He was parked behind the barn, and as he climbed into his late model BMW, a gleaming silver truck pulled up alongside him. Wondering who was visiting the barn so late, he was surprised to see Matt Montgomery and his border collie.

"Hi," Patrick said with a wave. "Are you looking for me?"

"Uh, no, I found Dusty Anderson's check."

"She'll be very pleased to hear that. She was just telling me about it. I think she's with her horse."

"Thanks. See you later."

As the BMW drove away, Matt climbed from his truck and wandered into the barn. Poking his head into the tack room he found it empty, so ambled down the barn aisle, his footfalls quiet in the soft dirt. He could hear the murmuring of a soft, female voice coming from one of the stalls, and as he reached it, he peered through the bars. Dusty was combing her horse's mane.

"Dot Anderson?" he said softly, "though I guess you prefer Dusty these days."

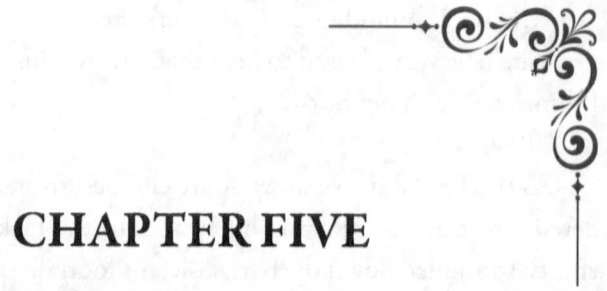

CHAPTER FIVE

DUSTY DIDN'T RESPOND.

"I have something I think is yours," Dylan continued, wishing she'd stop grooming her horse and talk to him.

"What's that?"

"Your check. You must have dropped it when— uh—you must have dropped it earlier."

"Oh, thanks, I've been looking for it. You can leave it in the tack room if you want."

She still hadn't walked around her gelding to speak with him, and her voice sounded weak. She bore no resemblance to the furious spitfire with whom he'd done battle.

"Dusty—Dot—I don't know which name you prefer, but—"

"Dusty," she said quickly, interrupting him.

"Dusty, are you all right?"

"I just won the year end championship. What could possibly be wrong?"

"You tell me," he answered softly, "or tell Jinxy here. I'm sure he'd be happy to listen."

"Jinxy is with you?"

"Jinx is always with me," he replied, then taking a breath, he asked, "Are you gonna celebrate your victory tonight?"

"My mom and Aunt Sharon are taking me somewhere for dinner," she said, raising her head above her horse's neck.

"Dusty," he began, searching for the right words, "I'd really like a chance to start over. How would you feel about me takin' the three of you to The Sunset Lodge?"

"The Sunset Lodge?" she softly repeated.

"Would that be okay? We can go somewhere else if you'd like."

"Uh, no. The Sunset Lodge sounds great."

"Is that a yes?"

"I appreciate the invitation, but, uh, it feels kinda weird. I mean, after what happened."

"Let's put that behind us, at least for tonight. You and your horse were spectacular and I'd really like to help you celebrate," he said earnestly, then risking a little levity, he added, "With your mom and aunt there, we'll both have to be on our best behavior."

"Well...that's true," Dusty agreed, tilting up her chin and showing him a small smile. "Thanks. It's really nice of you to offer, but I should call mom and ask her. My phone is in the tack room."

"No time like the present," he pressed, sliding open the stall door. "The thing is, the manager at the lodge is a friend of mine and I can always get a table, but with the show in town they're busy every night."

"Okay, I'll try her now."

Though she moved out of the stall she kept her eyes lowered, but Jinx barked, demanding her attention.

"He's not gonna let you go anywhere without sayin' hello," Matt said with a chuckle.

"Jinxy," she murmured, crouching down to pet him. "You're the cutest collie ever. Do you want to come to the tack room with me? Come on, let's go call mom."

Cautiously optimistic, Matt began to close the door, but he suddenly spotted a patch of white between her horse's front legs. Stepping forward, he took a closer look.

A chill shivered down his spine.

Quickly stepping from the stall, he saw Dusty walking down the barn aisle, her bountiful backside poured into tight jeans. The gelding fell to the back of his mind as he pictured her bent over and naked, except for the hot pink chaps framing her gorgeous ass. But the spell was broken as she turned into the tack room. Wanting to give her some privacy, he wandered outside, only to find a truck and trailer rolling towards the barn. As it pulled slowly to a stop, a young cowboy jumped from the cab and opened the back doors ready for loading.

"My mom said that would be lovely, and thank you."

Matt turned around.

Dusty was standing a few feet behind him, and he understood why she'd kept her head lowered. Her eyes were puffy and red-rimmed, evidence of recent tears.

"Dusty, how old is Licorice?" he asked, pretending not to notice.

"The vet thinks around eleven, maybe twelve."

"Hey, Dusty? Is Licorice ready?" the driver of the truck asked as he approached.

"Hi, Jeb. Yep, I'll go get him. Matt, thanks ever so much for the invitation. What time should we be there?"

"Seven o'clock?"

"That sounds perfect. I'll see you then."

"Wait! Your check."

"Oh, right, thanks."

As she walked away with the driver, he stared after her, recalling the shy, scrawny teenager who barely spoke and was usually wearing baggy dungarees. It was still hard to believe Dot and Dusty were the same person. Calling to Jinx, he strode to his truck and opened the door. His dog leapt inside, and Matt climbed behind the wheel.

"Whatta ya know, Jinx! It looks like I've got a second shot," he declared, starting up the engine. "If dinner goes well tonight, I'll call her and make plans to take her out to lunch. I'm gonna make her listen to my side of the story, even if I have to put her over my knee to do it."

INSIDE THE BARN, DUSTY heard Matt's truck crunch against the gravel as he drove off. Slipping a halter on Licorice, she led him from his stall and out to the trailer. Her tender backside rubbed against her jeans, and she was aching to get home and peel them off.

"Jeb, I'll follow you," she said, walking Licorice around the trailer and loading him.

"Sounds good," the young man replied, closing up the back doors.

As she moved to her car and slid behind the wheel, she winced, then shook her head.

"That will go down as the most embarrassing moment of my life," she grunted. "If Patrick wasn't gay I would've been totally freaked out."

But her mind unexpectedly flashed back to the comment Matt had made.

You know what you need? An old-fashioned spankin'.

A swathe of fluttering butterflies burst to life in her stomach, and as she began to follow the trailer, the thought of Matt doing what Patrick had just done sent a hot flood between her legs.

THE SUNSET LODGE WAS a log cabin restaurant set above a lake. It was a twenty-minute drive from the small ranch where Dusty lived with her parents, but Matt was a mere five minutes away. His father lived in the small lakeside suburb, and wanting to be near him when his health began to fail, Matt had sold his condominium in town and bought a home a couple of blocks away. He didn't mind the drive into work every day, and enjoyed the serenity when he returned in the evenings. Most importantly, he was on hand if his father or mother needed him.

Arriving at the restaurant early, he settled at the busy bar to have a drink. As the Jack Daniels started to take the edge off, he thought about the horse Dusty called Licorice, but a moment later, his attention was pulled away as his guests walked in.

Dusty's svelte, willowy frame was draped in an aqua dress. With her intense green eyes and long blonde hair, he thought she resembled Darryl Hannah, but prettier than the famous actress. Her mother, Karen, wasn't tall like her daughter, but was very attractive and carried a sparkle in her eye. Not knowing Sharon King was Dusty's aunt, it was a happy surprise, and helped to break the ice. They were shown to a window table, and the view of the lake was breathtaking.

"This is very generous of you, Matt," Karen said gratefully, "and Tom, Dot's father, wanted me to thank you as well."

"He's out of town?" Matt asked.

"He's a long-haul driver. He's on his way back from the other side of the country right now."

"He must be very proud."

"He is. It hasn't been an easy road for either of our children, but they have risen to life's challenges. Brian, our son, is pre-med, and it looks as if our girl here could be a national champion."

"Don't count the chickens, mom," Dusty interjected. "You know I'm superstitious about that stuff."

As they perused their menus, Matt noticed Dusty was shifting in her seat, and a warm blush had fired her cheeks a delightful pink. He knew the symptoms. Had her butt been warmed? Did she have a man in her life? He didn't want to consider the idea, but it wouldn't surprise him. She was a knockout.

As the evening continued, Sharon shared endless gossip about the show, and her mother continued to call her Dot, which he could see Dusty found annoying. Not wanting to offend either of them he refrained from using any name at all.

"Licorice is such an athletic, talented horse," Matt remarked as dessert and coffee were served. "How did you find him?"

"He was by himself in a field across the street from where one of the barn kids lives. He looked so sad and skinny, I just couldn't stand it."

"She can be a bit impulsive," Sharon declared. "She just walked up to the front door and knocked. The woman there said she could just take him."

"You're kiddin'! Did this woman tell you anything about him?" Matt asked, leaning forward as he spoke. "Where he came from? Anything at all?"

"She was very close-lipped, wasn't she, honey," Karen replied. "We couldn't really afford a horse, what with Dot starting college and Rob wanting to be a doctor, but she promised she'd get a job to help pay for him and do all the work. She was true to her word. We already had Itsy and Bitsy, so he wouldn't be by himself."

"Itsy and Bitsy?" Matt repeated with a grin. "Who are Itsy and Bitsy?"

"Our goats," Dusty replied. "We got them so dad wouldn't have to keep dealing with an overgrown lawn when he'd come home. Licorice hit it off with them the minute he walked into the field."

"How long ago was that?"

"Let's see, about four, maybe five years?" Karen said thoughtfully. "Would that be right, Dot?"

"Something like that, but he looks completely different now. I have pictures. You wouldn't believe he's the same horse, and the way he took to barrel racing was crazy. Like he was born to it."

Matt suppressed a grin. The horse was just like her. She looked nothing like the skinny, timid girl who used to hang around the cafe and play with Jinx.

"Did you get a bill of sale?" he continued.

"Um, I can't remember. I'm not sure. Did we mom?"

"No, dear, I don't think so. Patrick might have. He's the one who spoke to the woman when he picked him up with you."

"He loaded into that trailer like he couldn't wait to get out of there," Dusty said wistfully. "The horse Gods were smiling on both of us that day."

"Do you have anyone interested in sponsoring you after the nationals? Are you interested in the pro-rodeo circuit?"

"Me? Lord, no. I may have won the division, but this is the first year I've come this far."

"Would you allow Silver Streak Saddles to throw their hat in the ring?"

"My goodness," Karen said, catching her breath. "That's such a generous offer."

But Dusty eyed him warily.

"What does that entail?" she asked. "I don't know much about sponsorship."

"Oh, you should do it," Sharon piped up. "I've known Matt and his father for ages. They won't mess you around."

"Every sponsorship deal is different," Matt began. "For starters, after the nationals you'd be given a custom made saddle with our logo on it, but it be would yours to keep. Quite frankly, I think it's the best saddle on the market. In the meantime, we'd fit you out with a saddle that would have no suggestion of our name, but I suspect your racin' times would improve."

"Honey, that old saddle of yours must be replaced," Sharon declared. "You were just saying so the other day."

"Obviously once you were on the circuit we'd cover all your travel expenses," Matt continued, "and you already have a brand wearin' those hot pink chaps. We can use that to market you, and Licorice as well. You could even be a spokesmodel for us if you wanted to be once things got rollin'."

"Me?" Dusty gasped. "A model?"

"Sure. We tailor our sponsorship deals to fit the individual, what they want as well as what we want. The first thing though, would be to fit you and Licorice for a saddle, and if we're gonna do that it has to be right away. They aren't made overnight."

"I don't know what to say," Dusty said slowly. "I mean, I didn't expect anything like this. I'm really flattered. Are you sure? I mean, I'm a nobody."

"I wouldn't call someone who just blitzed the competition all summer a nobody. Not only do you have truckloads of talent, you're a very attractive young woman. Silver Streak Saddles would benefit from bein' associated with you. Maybe we could look at the ins and outs of an advance. I'm not sure how that would affect your amateur status, but I suspect we could figure something out."

"Please say yes, sweetheart," Karen said softly. "You'd have a real shot at a great future."

Dusty stared at her mother.

She was right.

The financial burden of traveling to the national finals had been worrying them both. Though Patrick paid her a salary, the cost of attending the finals would be a heavy weight, and her saddle was old. She'd done her best to pad it effectively, but she knew it didn't offer Licorice the comfort he needed to perform his best.

"I'll say yes, on the condition that we go through the details with Patrick," Dusty finally said. "I've never done anything like this before. It's not that I don't appreciate the offer," she added hastily, "I do, very much, but I—"

"Say no more," Matt said raising his palm. "I was gonna ask if there was a professional you could talk to about this. Patrick would be ideal."

"This is wonderful," Karen exclaimed. "Matt, thank you!"

"I'll come out tomorrow and fit Licorice myself, but I'll have Kevin with me. He's my best man."

Dusty smiled and nodded, suddenly not trusting herself to speak. A wave of emotion had turned her throat hot. She'd soon be riding in a brand new saddle tailor-made for Licorice, and her financial stress might be coming to an end. She'd struggled for so long, the thought was overwhelming.

"How does two o'clock sound?"

"Good," she managed, "that sounds good."

"Excellent. Then it's settled."

Dusty swallowed back the hot, achy lump. It had been an emotional day. Her bottom was still scratchy, and every time she looked across the table at Matt, she was filled with the familiar need to feel his arms around her, and his lips against hers.

But now she hungered for something else as well.

More than anything, for some unfathomable reason, she wanted him to spank her.

CHAPTER SIX

KAREN COULDN'T WAIT to call her husband with the exciting news. Their financial burden was being lifted, and Sharon was convinced her niece would be a star, but sitting in the back seat on the drive home Dusty barely heard their chatter. Her mind was spinning.

Had Matt made the offer because he was interested in her romantically, or was a professional involvement his only motivation? Had he searched out who she was because she'd won, or did he remember she was Dot Anderson of his own accord? As the car turned into the driveway she decided it didn't matter. She'd have a new saddle and far less worry about money.

Sharon headed home, and Dusty and her mother hurried inside to call her father. He was ecstatic, and promised they'd have a celebration when he returned.

"Thanks, dad. I never thought anything like this would ever happen to me."

"You've worked hard. You deserve every bit of it!" he replied. "I'll see you soon. I love you, kitten."

"I love you too, dad."

Ending the call, Dusty moved to the kitchen window and gazed out at the horse that had made it all possible.

"He's something special," her mother sighed, walking up to join her. "The way he performs for you is just remarkable, but you rescued him and nursed him back to health. He knows you saved him."

"I love him so much, and not just because he's so talented, but because of how we are together. The way he looks at me is...I can't describe it. I can hear him talking to me, I swear I can."

"You two are a match. Let's hope you find a man as special as Licorice."

Immediately thinking of Matt, she kissed her mother goodnight and ambled into her bedroom. As she undressed and cleaned off her makeup, she wondered how many girls the wealthy saddle-maker had at his beck and call. Climbing into bed and closing her eyes, she sent her fingers between her legs, picturing him surrounded by his beautiful saddles. As the scene began to play itself out, her fingers danced urgently against her clit.

"I told you, no hissy fits. I made that real clear little lady, and now I'm gonna spank you. Maybe if your bottom is stingin' for a while you'll get the message."

"I'm a grown woman. You have no right to treat me this way."

"I have every right. You're the face of Silver Streak Saddles and you need to remember that," he declared, bending her over the wide seat of a chestnut colored saddle on a display stand. *"When you misbehave it reflects on this company. I'm not havin' it."*

The seat wrapped around her, but his smacks stung, and she wriggled as they continued to land on the same spot.

"I'm sorry, Matt, I'll be really good, I promise."

"Sir, you'll call me Sir when I'm whippin' your butt."

The fantasy felt real.

She could even smell the leather.

Her fingers rubbed furiously, and as the spasms shuddered through her limbs, tears spilled from her eyes.

I want him so badly. I've wanted him my whole life. Nothing has changed.

───────── ❧ ─────────

LEAVING THE SUNSET Lodge, Matt had been grateful for his jacket. It wasn't a chilly evening, but cool enough to warrant him slipping it on and closing the buttons. He'd been fighting a growing erection, and during the conversation about the sponsorship offer he'd lost the battle.

As they'd discussed the details, he'd been sinking into the deep green of Dusty's eyes, and occasionally glimpsed her sharp nipples under the thin fabric of her dress. When he'd talked about fitting the saddle the following day, he imagined watching her bottom as she rode, and his cock had sprung to full attention.

Though he lived only a few minutes from The Sunset Lodge, driving home hadn't been easy.

He kept picturing her on all fours wearing her hot pink chaps, her naked ass blushing from the smacks of his hand, her legs separated, her pussy glistening, and her long blonde hair falling across her back.

Pulling into his garage and stepping into his kitchen, Jinx greeted him excitedly, but Matt moved swiftly to his bedroom and hurriedly stripped off. Throwing himself on the bed, he wrapped his fingers around his cock and urgently stroked. The orgasm began building almost immediately, and though he tried to milk the moment, the need was too great. With the lascivious images drifting through his mind, he exploded with a powerful release.

His heart pounding, he closed his eyes and let out a heavy breath.

As he recovered, he considered calling one of his female friends to make plans for the following night. Seeing Dusty in the afternoon would set him on fire again, but as the idea of the casual hookup took hold, a frown crossed his brow.

It didn't feel right.

"I'm just tired," he grunted. "I'll call Lucy in the mornin'."

Satisfied, he ambled toward the bathroom, stopped to pat Jinx and let him know he was still loved, then stood under a quick shower. But a short time later as he fell into bed, he knew he wouldn't be calling Lucy or any other girl in the morning, and he fleetingly wondered why.

THOUGH MATT HAD OVERSLEPT and was hurrying to get to work, he had to see his father. As he'd stirred from sleep, Matt had wondered if his offer of sponsorship might have been unwise. And there was the matter of Dusty's horse.

"How did things suddenly get so complicated?" he muttered, pulling into the driveway of his parent's home.

The house was a single story, rambling ranch house overlooking the lake. Letting himself in, he could hear his mother humming in the kitchen. He smiled. It meant his father was doing well.

"Hey, mom," he called, striding into the kitchen and pecking her on the cheek as Jinx barked his greeting.

"This is a lovely surprise. Would you like some breakfast?"

"That sounds great. Thanks. I take it dad had a good night?"

"Your dad has had several good nights," she said happily. "Of course, he always sleeps well after a day at Silver Streak. It's good for him."

"I think so too. He seems like his old self when he's there," Matt said, pouring himself a mug of coffee. "Is he in the den?"

"He said something about tinkering in his workshop," she replied, then studying her son, she tilted her head to the side. "Matt...you seem to have a twinkle in your eye. A twinkle and worry. Have you met someone? Is it serious?"

"The girl or the worry?"

"Aren't they one and the same?"

"Kinda. Do you remember Dot Anderson?"

"That sweet girl who never seemed to grow up? Skinny as a rail and—Matt! Is that who you're talking about?"

"Yep, and she has grown up! Big time," Matt exclaimed. "She's turned into a helluva barrel racer. She's goin' to the nationals. I've offered to sponsor her if she turns pro, and I'm gonna fit her horse this afternoon. I'd like to date her, but I want Silver Streak to back her as well."

"Ah, I understand. You're worried about potential problems down the road."

"Exactly."

"Sometimes you can have your cake and eat it too, just lay down some ground rules real quick. No skulduggery. Make sure everything is out in the open, and the contract gives you both an easy out. No-one likes to feel trapped."

"I was thinkin' the same thing, no secrets, but an easy out clause is a good idea. Why didn't I think of it? Jeez!"

"If someone had come to you with the same problem, you would have. It's always harder to see the obvious when you're too close."

"No kiddin'," he muttered, shaking his head. "Thanks, mom."

"You're welcome, honey."

"I'm gonna go find pop."

"If you're taking that coffee with you, don't spill it on my rug."

"Um, I think I'll leave it here," he said with a grin, and taking a long swallow, he left the mug on the counter. "Jinx, are you comin'?"

"He's not going anywhere as long as this bacon is frying."

"Yeah, you're right about that!"

Heading to his father's workshop, Matt flashed back to Dusty's unfathomable green eyes gazing back at him the night before. He wanted to believe the intense attraction was mutual, but if he was wrong, would he screw everything up by asking her out?

"Hey, pop."

"Matt, come on in," his father said, looking up from his work bench. "You look like you've got somethin' on your mind."

"I need to talk to you about a horse."

WHEN DUSTY CALLED PATRICK to share the exciting news, he'd been thrilled, and promised to swing by during the saddle fitting. Her mother worked as a secretary, and with her morning free Dusty had promised to do the weekly shopping. She was about to leave when the house phone rang. When she picked it up and heard Matt's voice, her pulse quickened.

"Is everything okay?" she asked. "Are you still coming this afternoon?"

"Yes, I am, but I need to talk with you before then. Is there any chance you could swing by my office? I'm on Henderson Street."

"Sure, I was just on my way in."

"It's the grey buildin' at the end of the block. You can't miss it. There's a large sign, Silver Streak Saddlery, with a saddle underneath the name."

"I'll stop in before I go to the store. Is fifteen minutes okay?"

"Yep, that's great. See you then."

"Bye," she replied cheerily, but hanging up the phone, she couldn't help but wonder why he needed to see her. "Don't borrow trouble," she muttered, and letting out a breath, she picked up her bag and headed to her car.

Climbing behind the wheel and starting off, her wicked fantasy from the night before floated into her head. It was unsettling, but by the time she reached the end of Henderson Street she'd managed to calm herself.

"Deep breaths!" she muttered as she parked. "He probably needs me to pick out colors or something. This will be fun."

But walking through the double doors into the reception area, she caught her breath.

Life-sized horses stood on synthetic grass, each wearing a saddle more beautiful than the next. Oversized photographs of barrel racing, team penning and rodeo scenes graced the walls, and a portrait of Matt's father hung behind the reception desk.

"You must be Dusty," the woman behind the front desk piped up. "Matt told me you'd be arriving."

"Yes, I am," Dusty replied, still taking it all in.

"I'll page him. There's a coffee bar behind the Palomino if you care for a drink."

"Thank you."

Though she didn't want anything, Dusty couldn't resist taking a peek to see what the coffee bar offered. Walking behind the golden horse, she found a machine offering everything from espresso to latte's, and a refrigerator with sodas and bottled water. Two glass jars held individually wrapped chocolate-chip and oatmeal-raisin cookies.

Something suddenly touched her leg.

Startled, she jumped away, then stared down to find Jinx beside her.

"Jinxy," she exclaimed, leaning down to pet him. "You'd make a great cat burglar."

"He prefers to chase them rather than steal them," Matt said with a chuckle.

"I'm sure," she replied, straightening up. "This is like a self-serve coffee shop."

"We have quite a few visitors, but it's for the people who work here as well. Come on in. I'll take you to my office via the scenic route."

"The scenic route?"

"Through the workroom where the magic happens."

"You mean where the saddles are made?"

"Yep. There are guys workin' here that started with dad, and they're magicians, but we won't stop and talk. They'll never let you leave. Next time you can visit with them if you want."

With Jinx leading the way, they had walked through a door that opened into a wide hallway. Stopping at the entrance to the workroom, Matt punched in his code, slid in his card key, then pushed open the heavy steel door.

"Oh...my...gosh," Dusty breathed. "This is amazing!"

"Keep walkin," he chuckled. "Even I have trouble if I stop. My eyes get glued on something and I can't pull them away."

"I'm not surprised," she mumbled, staring at a row of stunning silver ornaments.

The floor was concrete, exactly as she'd imagined it, and a chestnut saddle sat proudly on display. She suddenly saw herself bent across it, her ass naked, waiting for his hard hand.

"Almost there," he said, snatching her from the salacious thought.

"Uh-huh," she muttered, the simple response all she could manage.

Reaching the end of the room, he led her up a staircase, down a short hallway, and sliding a key into a lock he opened his office door.

"You have so much security."

"It's essential. Let's go out to my patio. It's private there, and quiet," he said, moving across the room and opening a door with frosted glass.

The patio had high walls on either side, and overlooked a forest. A wrought iron table offered four chairs and an umbrella, and a pair of loungers sat against the far wall, one covered by a fuzzy blanket. Jinx immediately trotted over and jumped on it.

"When I have to do anything technical I come out here," Matt said, pulling out a chair for her at the table. "This is also where I read contracts. Surrounded by the trees helps me concentrate."

"Forgive me for saying this," she said as she sat down, "but I thought this place would be like an oversized shoe repair shop. "

"That's how it was when my father started the company."

"He should be very proud."

"Hard work and long hours paid off," he replied, settling across the table.

"But he must be a very smart guy."

"Oh, yes," Matt said with a grin. "As smart as they come."

"So... why am I here?"

"You're here because I need to ask you about, uh, what happened between us at the show ground, and there's somethin' important I need to tell you."

"I can only imagine," she quipped, rolling her eyes. "Where do you want to start?"

CHAPTER SEVEN

WHEN MATT HAD WALKED into the reception area and seen Dusty's curvaceous backside so perfectly encased in her thin white slacks, he had an immediate rush of energy through his loins. Now sitting across the table, her green eyes sparkling and the hint of her cleavage peeking over her blouse, he was having a difficult time concentrating.

"What's the matter, Matt?"

"There's nothin' the matter," he said quickly.

"So...do you want to know why I was angry, or would you prefer to start with whatever it is you need to tell me?"

"Uh, the first thing, I mean, why you were so upset?" he replied, willing himself to focus.

"Why do you think?"

"If I knew I wouldn't be askin.'"

She took a breath, promising herself not to get angry again.

"You didn't remember me, and I used to run into you all the time," she declared. "On top of that, it seemed you only wanted to talk to me because my appearance has changed, not because I might have something worthwhile to offer."

"You've got to be kiddin' me!" he retorted. "People are attracted to each other for all kinds of reasons, and physical attraction is a big part of that. If you didn't find a guy physically attractive, would you go out with him?"

Dusty squirmed. He had a point.

"I'll take that as a no," he said firmly. "As far as rememberin' you, good grief, girl, you were just a high-school kid with braces and glasses, not that there's anything wrong with that," he added hastily. "Besides, back then I was in college. If I wasn't studyin' I was workin' here with my dad, and I'd only see you for a couple of minutes when I'd zip into the cafe for a coffee run. And by the way, I tried real hard to make friends with you, but I'd barely say two words and you'd run off."

She suddenly found herself at a loss for words.

He was right.

She remembered blushing beet red and hurrying away.

"That hissy fit you threw at me yesterday was unwarranted," he continued. "Why didn't you just talk to me? When I said you needed a spankin', I wasn't kiddin'."

Embarrassed, she dropped her eyes and she stared at her hands.

"I'm sorry, Matt. I don't know what else to say."

"Apology accepted," he said, softening his voice. "We all have our moments."

"What was the other thing you wanted to talk to me about?" she asked, a pink blush crossing her cheeks.

"I'd like to ask you to dinner, but I don't want you to think that's why I made the sponsorship offer, and I don't want any kinda weirdness. If you don't wanna go out with me, no problem, the offer still stands. It has no strings."

Her heart leapt.

Matthew Montgomery, the guy she'd dreamed about since the first moment she'd laid eyes on him had just asked her out.

"So, whatta ya say? Can I take you to dinner?"

"Sure," she managed. "Uh, why are you looking at me like that?"

He had leaned across the table, his eyes had narrowed, and he was staring at her with an impenetrable gaze.

Matt had made a decision.

He was about to roll the dice.

"Dusty," he murmured, "I'm gonna kiss you, then I'm gonna hug you, then I'm gonna smack your butt. You don't have a problem with any of that, do you?"

"Smack me?"

"Yep, just a bit, for that tantrum you threw. We've gotta start off on the right foot, and hissy fits, they don't fly with me."

"But, uh, here?"

Ignoring her question, his fingers slipped in her hair, and gripping it firmly, he pressed his lips urgently against hers.

Dusty's heart pounded like a hammer driving home a long, thick nail, her stomach churned, and every nerve in her body sparked. As he broke away, rose from his chair and pulled her into his arms, she sank against him, barely able to stand without his support.

"Girl, you are so gorgeous," he muttered, engulfing her in a tight, enveloping hug. "Now I'm gonna spank you."

A thousand butterflies burst to life.

With one arm tightly around her waist, his free hand roamed over her backside. She squeezed her eyes shut as he landed his first swat, and when he delivered the second, her pelvis thrust forward of its own accord. His rigid cock was suddenly against her, and she dug her fingers into his back as the third swat made her gasp.

"Just a few more," he mumbled, "a bit harder."

The thin cotton of her white slacks provided little protection, and when his hard hand delivered a flurry of stinging smacks, she clutched his shirt and buried her head in his shoulder.

"Are you gonna be a good girl now? No more tantrums?"

"Yes, I'll be a good girl," she softly bleated. "No more tantrums, but, uh, I can't believe I let you do that."

"You wanted me to," he said softly.

Slowly lifting her head, she stared into his eyes.

"I want to tell you...uh..." she paused, searching for the words.

"Go on."

"I, uh, used to have a crush on you. That's why I was so upset you didn't remember me."

"Then it's just as well I was busy back then, and you didn't look like you do now."

"Why would you say that?"

"Because I'd be in jail, that's why. There's such a thing as legal age."

"Oh, yeah, I guess you're right."

"Okay, Miss Hot Pink Chaps, I think I'd better send you on your way or I won't get any work done. I'll be at your house at two-o'clock, and we'll see about gettin' you squared away with a decent saddle."

"Patrick said he'll try to be there. I hope that's okay."

"That's better than okay. I was gonna ask you to call him and see if he could join us. Come on, Jinx, let's see this lovely lady out."

Jumping off his lounger, Jinx trotted past them to the door.

"I still can't believe you just did that," she muttered, her face still flaming, "and I still can't believe I let you."

"It won't be the last time," he promised as they left his office.

"Don't say that!"

But she didn't meant it.

Not for a second.

She couldn't wait to find herself naked and lying over his lap.

THE REMAINDER OF THE morning flew by. After grocery shopping and tidying the house, Dusty cleaned up Licorice's shelter then began grooming him. Now Matt was due to arrive at any minute. With his black coat glowing in the sun, and a glossy sheen to his thick mane and tail, Licorice looked every bit the show champion he was. Heading back into the house, Dusty started the coffee, opened a packet of ready-to-bake chocolate chip cookie dough, sliced off the sections and popped them in the oven.

Hurrying to her room, she quickly peeled off her blouse and pulled on a v-neck, pink T-shirt. As she made her way back down the hall, she heard a truck roll into the driveway. Quickening her step to the front door, she opened it to find Matt already walking up the path with an older man at his side.

"Hi, Matt."

"Hey, Dusty," he said, pecking her on the cheek. "This is Kevin. Kevin, this is Dusty Anderson."

"Real nice to meet you," the grizzled cowboy said, smiling as he extended his hand.

He looked to be in his sixties, but when Dusty shook his hand she was shocked by the smoothness of his skin.

"Hi, Kevin. Good to meet you too. Please come in. I have fresh coffee and chocolate chip cookies baking."

"Mmm, I can smell 'em," he remarked. "That's real nice of you."

"I have Jinx with me," Matt said, "but I wasn't sure if it would be okay to bring him in the house."

"Of course it is. I'd love to see him."

Matt marched back to his truck, and as he opened the passenger door, Jinx jumped from the cab and bounded up to her.

"Hey Jinxy," she said happily. "I'm so glad you're here."

Dropping his nose to the ground, Jinx sniffed his way past her, then followed her as she led Matt and Kevin through the kitchen and out to the patio.

"That's one fine lookin' horse," Kevin declared, studying Licorice on the other side of the fence that separated his paddock from the back yard.

"I won't argue with that," she said happily. "Um, Kevin, I hope you don't mind me mentioning this, but your hands are so soft."

"I get that a lot. It's from years of rubbing oils and conditioners into the leather, but my fingertips are calloused."

He stretched out his hand, and she could see the evidence of his work etched into the ends of his fingers.

"Wow. Do you know how many saddles you've made?"

"Nope, I lost count." he replied with a chuckle. "Let's go take a look at your boy."

Matt had stood back as Kevin and Dusty talked. He wanted to soak in the sight of her, and glancing at her full, round bottom, he wondered if she was still tender. The thought stirred his cock, but as they headed to the paddock he shifted his attention to the matter at hand. As they passed the feed room, Dusty ducked inside to fetch some carrots, handing them off as they entered the field. With Licorice gobbling up the treats, Kevin ran his hands over the horse's body.

"His right shoulder's a bit more developed than the left," Kevin remarked, taking a quick moment to glance between his front legs, "but that's not unusual."

"Why is that?" Dusty asked.

"Could be your saddle's been tweaking him a bit, not givin' him the freedom of movement there so he favors the right side. Horse's can fool a rider into doin' it his way, but it's not uncommon. Is there a back entrance? I've gotta bring my tools in."

"Yes, right over there," she replied, pointing to a gate that led from the backyard into the driveway.

"Matt, you wanna give me a hand?"

"Yep, sure thing."

"I need to get the cookies out of the oven," Dusty declared, feeding Licorice the last carrot.

Splitting up as they left the paddock, she walked into the house and Matt and Kevin left through the gate.

She didn't see the worried look that passed between them.

CHAPTER EIGHT

MATT AND KEVIN HAD arrived in separate vehicles. Kevin's van was outfitted with the equipment needed for his work, and Matt had driven his truck so he could stay after the fitting was completed. Kevin opened the side door of his van, then sat on the small amount of floor space available in front of a slide-out bench.

"I'm sorry to say it, but you were right, Matt," Kevin said gravely. "That's Black Lightnin'."

"Damn," Matt grimaced. "You're sure?"

"The owner flew me back east just to fit him. It was right before your dad started feelin' poorly."

"Whatta we do?"

"I reckon you've gotta have a pow-wow. Get your dad together with this Patrick fella you told me about, Dusty and her folks. I'm just a simple guy, but if Lightnin' was abandoned, and it sure seems like he was, anyone tryin' to stake a claim would have a tough job."

"That's what I think, but Dusty will be heartsick, and she's got the nationals comin' up."

"Maybe you can handle this without her knowin', but if she goes to the nationals someone is bound to recognize him."

"I have to find out how he ended up in that backyard."

"We should still have his file. Maybe there'll be somethin' there to give you a startin' point, and I've got some contacts back east that might know somethin' without causin' a ruckus, but you need to talk this out with your dad."

"How the hell did that horse end up here, all the way from New York?"

"Beats me," Kevin said shaking his head. "Let's get him fitted, and I'll make some calls when I get back."

Pulling the tools from the van, they headed back to the paddock where Dusty was waiting. Setting up his equipment, Kevin ran a thermal imaging device across the gelding's body and measured him with what appeared to be a steel replica of a horse's spinal column, all the while making copious notes. He'd just put down his pen and notebook when Patrick entered through the back gate and jogged towards them.

"Sorry I'm late," he apologized as he approached. "I got held up at the show."

"Not a problem, Patrick," Dusty said gratefully. "I'm glad you made it. "This is Kevin, and of course you know Matt."

"Your timin's perfect," Kevin declared. "I was just gonna show Dusty where her saddle doesn't fit. No amount of paddin' can make a saddle fit where it don't. Licorice has inflammation in both shoulders, but it's worse on the left, and some back soreness. His current saddle is too long."

"Licorice, I'm so sorry," Dusty muttered, hugging his neck.

"Hey, you didn't know," Matt said quickly. "I've seen a whole lot worse."

"I've got a few saddles with me," Kevin continued, "and one of them will see you through till yours is done, but don't go puttin' your old one on him again. Sell it, donate it, whatever."

"My gosh, I won't, not in a million years. I'll deliver it to the consignment store tomorrow."

"We can take all this equipment back to my van. I already know which saddle will be a good temporary."

"Thank you so much," Dusty said earnestly. "I can't believe he's performed so brilliantly."

"You just wait," Kevin said knowingly. "He's got a whole other speed just waitin'."

Kevin and Matt packed up the equipment, and with Patrick's help, they carried it through the backyard and loaded it into the van. As Kevin selected the saddle Dusty could use and carted it away, Matt pulled Patrick aside.

"Patrick, I know we've just met," he said solemnly, "and I hate to spring this on you, but there's a situation with Dusty's horse." "That sounds serious. What kind of situation?"

"Prepare yourself. Licorice is a champion barrel racer from New York called Black Lightenin'. His owner was a wealthy guy with a string of horses, and somehow Lightenin' ended up wastin' away in that back-yard where Dusty found him."

"I can't believe what I'm hearing. Are you're sure it's the same horse?"

"As sure as I can be!" Matt said solemnly. "Patrick, did you get a bill of sale when you picked him up?"

"I wrote one out," Patrick said thoughtfully. "I'm very particular about that kind of thing. I'll check the minute I get home. Give me your number and I'll call you."

"At least that's somethin'," Matt said with a sigh. "Let's try to keep this under wraps until we know more. No need upsettin' Dusty just yet."

"I agree. Do you think he'll be recognized if she goes to the nation-als?"

"It's a small world at the top, and Licorice is a unique lookin' horse. He's solid black with that white patch between his front legs, and he'll be registered."

"Shit," Patrick muttered. "We don't have much time."

"With some careful diggin' we can get the back story, then take it from there. The priority though, is to protect Dusty."

"I'll do whatever I can to help."

"Thanks, Patrick. I'll keep you posted."

"I need to get back to the show, but I always have my phone on me. Thanks for everything," Patrick said gratefully, climbing into his car. "Dusty deserves a break. She's worked her butt off to get where she is."

As Patrick drove off, Matt turned and saw Kevin walking up to his van.

"Is she all set?" Matt asked, moving quickly up to meet him.

"Yep. She sure does love that horse. I hope this story has a happy endin'."

"Me too. Thanks, Kevin. I'll see you back at work."

"I'll dig out that file. One way or another we'll figure this out."

"From your lips," Matt muttered as Kevin climbed into his van.

"Hey, Matt. Figure out what?" Dusty asked, walking up behind him.

"The decorative trim for your saddle," Matt said hastily watching Kevin back out of the driveway.

"Oh, right. I guess you'll need my ideas."

"You could just leave it to us and be surprised."

"I'll have to think about that. Do you want to go inside and have some coffee?"

"What I want, is some Dusty," he said with a grin, pulling her into his arms.

"I know that saddle Kevin left is just temporary, but it felt amazing," she said with a sigh, leaning against him. "I can't wait to ride in it, properly I mean, not just walk around and trot a bit."

"Was your butt a bit tender?"

"Stop it," she retorted, feeling a fresh blush crawl over her face.

"Nope. Answer the question."

"Yes, it is a bit."

Grabbing a fistful of hair, he tugged it back and stared down at her.

"It will be again, I can promise you that."

"What if I'm an especially good girl?" she whispered, trying to ignore the sudden burst of butterflies in her stomach.

"I'll still warm your backside."

"Why?"

"An ounce of prevention. Now quit talkin' and kiss me."

His voice was gruff, his eyes were filled with lust, and when he dropped his lips against hers, she could feel his hardness pressing against her.

"Matt," she mumbled as they broke apart, "it's like you...you..."

"What?" he asked, his voice a hoarse whisper.

"I can't explain it. This will sound corny, but when you kiss me, I swear, you set me on fire."

"Kinda goes both ways. Maybe we should have that coffee."

"Maybe we should," she breathed, wishing they could just fall on the ground and consume each other.

They headed into the kitchen, Jinx bounding across the yard to join them. Matt poured them both a cup while Dusty retrieved the creamer, sugar, and the plate of cookies.

"You still live here, with your folks," he asked, sitting at the table and wishing his cock would go back to sleep.

"Dad's always on the road, and Brian's away at school, so I stay here for mom. I don't mind. I couldn't afford much if I left, so it works for now."

"Can you come and go as you please? I mean, uh..."

"Are you asking me if I can stay out all night if I want?" she murmured, shooting him a sassy grin.

"I guess that was kinda clumsy."

"And here I thought you were such a smooth talker."

"Smooth talker? Hell, no, I'm just a simple cowboy."

"Yeah, about as simple as an algebra problem!"

"So, about tonight, I'll pick you up around seven. I'm taking you to a place that's about twenty minutes away. It has a view of the lake, and it has a really great chef."

"I didn't know there was another restaurant at the lake. Is it dressy, like The Sunset Lodge?"

"Um, you can dress however you want, though I am partial to skirts."

"What's the name of this place?"

"Matteo's."

It took a moment for the penny to drop, and when it did she began to laugh.

"Are you taking me to your house for dinner?"

"No, I told you, Matteo's," he replied with a straight face.

"It's your house. Don't you lie to me!"

"I'm not lying," he said with a grin. "Tonight my place is called Matteos, and the chef will be serving salmon in a lemon-dill sauce with saffron rice."

"Oh, my, gosh, are you serious? You're making that?"

"You'll just have to wait and see," he declared, rising from the table. "Now I'd best be goin'."

Slowly rising to her feet, Dusty slipped her arms around his neck and pressed herself against him.

"I'd be careful if I were you," he warned reaching his hands around to cup her bottom. "I might have a real hard time leavin' if you keep this up."

"But, Matt, I'm in need of a goodbye hug, and another kiss."

"I don't wanna spoil you."

"Spoil me," she softly insisted. "You can always spank me later."

"Damn, girl."

Unable to resist, he crushed his lips against hers, kissing her with lust-filled abandon until they were breathless. Her knees about to buckle, she fell against him.

"Now I am goin'," he panted, "and if you stop me again, I'll pick you up and throw you on to the first bed I find."

"That'll work," she stammered, "that'll work just fine."

"You, little lady, are definitely, gonna get spanked tonight, and you can take that to the bank."

"Why?" she murmured, finally pulling back and gazing up at him.

"Cos you're a siren! No, you're more than a siren. You're a siren in hot pink chaps, and you need a spankin'. Don't forget your toothbrush."

"You're taking a lot for granted, cowboy."

"Are you sayin' you won't bring your toothbrush?"

"I'm saying, you'll have to wait and see."

"Touche!" he said with a wicked grin. "Come on, Jinx, I think it's time we rolled."

Jinx had found a spot near the glass slider, and yawning, he sat up, stretched, shook his body, then slowly ambled over to them.

"I'll see you soon, Jinxy," Dusty said softly, leaning down to rub his head.

Matt took her hand as they headed down the hallway, and when he kissed her goodbye—a long, lingering warm kiss—she felt herself melt all over again.

"I'll see you tonight, beautiful girl."

"I'm really looking forward to it."

Closing the door behind him, she leaned against it and let out a sigh, then filled with longing, she moved to her bedroom, quickly pulled off her jeans, and falling on her bed, she pressed her fingers urgently against her sex. Closing her eyes she imagined herself lying naked with him, his hands exploring her body, tweaking her nipples, and his fingers whispering across her sex.

You, are definitely, gonna get spanked tonight, and you can take that to the bank.

His sexy threat floated through her head, abruptly sending her over the edge. As the shuddering climax rattled through her, she could feel the residual tenderness from his quick, sharp spanking at his office. Dropping her hand away she fell limp, and softly moaning, let herself drift into an easy nap.

CHAPTER NINE

WHEN MATT PULLED INTO the driveway of Dusty's house a few minutes after seven, he couldn't recall the last time he'd felt so nervous. He'd even taken a swig of whiskey before leaving his home, and had to brush his teeth a second time. He'd thought about buying flowers, changed his mind, then stopped at a grocery story on the way and picked up a bouquet of various blooms wrapped in yellow cellophane with a large satin bow. Sitting in his truck, he stared at the flowers lying on the passenger seat next to him.

"Too much? Not enough? Is it cheesy?" he muttered. "Since when did it stop bein' okay for a guy to bring a girl flowers on their first date?"

He may have felt less stressed if he'd known that Dusty was just as anxious. Nothing she'd taken from her closet was right. The skirt was too long or too shirt, the shirt was too tight, or not tight enough, and she'd finally settled on the very first dress she'd picked out.

Crimping her eyelashes with a curler, she smudged her mascara as she attempted to apply it to the very tips of her lashes. Cursing under her breath she painstakingly removed the black mark with a cotton swab, trying not to make it worse, and when the doorbell rang she almost shoved the swab into her eye missing it by centimeters.

"I'll get it," her mother called.

Pulling on her pink cardigan, she thought it would compliment the black dress dotted with tiny pink tulips, but staring at her reflection, she groaned.

"Now I look twelve years old!" she muttered under her breath. "Screw it. It's too late to change."

Picking up her handbag and moving down the hall, she heard Matt and her mother talking in the living room. Pausing to take a deep breath and settle her nerves, she walked in.

"Matt brought you some flowers," her mother beamed. "Isn't it wonderful that some men still know how to treat a woman?"

"Thank you," Dusty said with a smile, but more because she wondered what mother would have to say if she knew what Matt had done on the patio of his office. "I'm an old-fashioned kinda guy," Matt said, handing Dusty the bouquet. "I hope that sits okay with you, Dusty."

"It sits with me just fine."

"I'll put them in a vase," her mother suggested, taking them from Dusty. "You two have a lovely evening, and don't worry about waking me when you get in. I'll be dead to the world. I plan on an early night."

"Thanks, mom," Dusty said as her mother left the room.

"You look very pretty in that dress," Matt said as they started towards the front door. "Thank you, you don't look so bad yourself," she replied, suddenly feeling like the awkward young teenager that used to hang around the cafe.

Stepping outside, Matt walked her up to the passenger door, opened it for her, then hurried around and climbed in behind the wheel. "How did you become such a terrific rider?" he asked, starting up the truck. "You totally outclassed the other competitors I saw."

"Just hours in the saddle, I guess. Riding was all I had growing up, and Patrick let me work at the barn in exchange for training. When I told mom and dad I wanted to be a horse professional they were all for it. Going to school at the County Agricultural College I could stay at home and continue riding with Patrick. I couldn't afford my own horse, which was tough, but then I found Licorice! He was like a gift from God. I would never have been able to compete at the level I'm at now without him."

"Was Licorice his name when you got him?"

"No, the woman called him Knight. I'm surprised she called him anything. She had no idea how to take care of a horse, but at least she kept him shod. I guess that's something."

"Why did she have him? Did she give you any information?"

"She said she'd promised to look after him for a month or so for a friend, but the friend disappeared, so she just kept him. I don't know why. She had no saddle, nothing. He was like some kind of backyard ornament. Do you ride? You must, surely."

"Yep, I keep my horse over at Circus Farms. Jackson is his name. I ride early in the mornin' and on the weekends. I'd like to take you over there sometime. It's just on the other side of the hill where you live."

"I know Circus Farms. I look down on it when I ride to the top of that hill, and I'd love to meet Jackson."

Though the conversation between them was easy and comfortable, subtle electricity danced in the air, and when Matt rolled his truck into his garage, a sudden rush of nerves sent Dusty's heart racing.

"Matteo's Restaurant!" Matt declared with a grin. "I hope the food is to your liking."

"You really made salmon with a sauce and saffron rice? Did you wear a frilly pink apron or a big chef's hat?"

"Keep on bein' sassy," he retorted, climbing from the truck. "You're just givin' me more reason to spank your cute tush."

"But, Matt, you've already told me you don't need an excuse."

He chuckled, then walked around to open her door. "It's real nice to have you here," he said softly, and as his hand wrapped around hers to help her out, he leaned in and kissed her.

It wasn't the kiss that took her breath away. It wasn't how delicious his lips felt, or how warmly he kissed her, it was that the kiss was completely spontaneous. "Welcome to my home," he whispered, moving his lips to her ear.

"You can welcome me to your home any time you want," she breathed, wanting to fall into his arms and never leave them.

Still holding her hand he led her through the door. Jinx was standing in the kitchen eagerly waiting, and when he saw Dusty his excitement bubbled over.

"He sure is happy to see you," Matt said with a laugh as his dog barked and danced around her.

"The feeling's mutual. Wow, something smells really good."

"That's apple crumble. I took it out of the oven before I left to pick you up." "You're kidding? You're an impressive man, Mr. Montgomery."

"You can thank my mom. She said a woman likes a man who can cook, not that my dad could. I think she wanted to be sure I didn't starve when I left home."

"She sounds like a smart lady. It also meant you wouldn't be on her doorstep begging for food."

"I hadn't thought of that! How about I give you a tour of the house, maybe have some wine, then we can eat?"

"Sounds perfect."

With Jinx happily running beside them, he took her through the living room out to the patio that overlooked the lake, then showed her his den and the guest room, but as they approached the double doors that led into his bedroom, he paused.

"I should warn you, this is more than just a bedroom. I knocked out the wall to the second guest room."

"Sounds great. Are you going to show me or just stand there and tell me about it?"

"I wanted to give you a head's up," he replied, and then pushed open the doors.

Dusty caught her breath.

At the far end of the room, a grouping of furniture faced a floor to ceiling, natural rock fireplace. French doors led out to a wide patio with a spectacular view of the lake. Bronzes of horses sat in bookcases with other nicknacks, beautifully framed paintings of westerns scenes graced the walls, and thick fluffy rugs were placed strategically on the dark, hardwood floor. As she took it all in, her eyes came to rest on the king-sized brass bed.

"So?" he asked, wondering why it was suddenly so important that she liked his renovations.

"I think this is the most beautiful bedroom I've ever seen in my life," she breathed, wandering across to the bed. "This bed is incredible."

He moved behind her, and lifting her hair off her neck, he laid his lips against her skin. Moaning softly, she tilted her head to the side inviting more. Sliding his hands to her shoulders, he slowly slid her cardigan down her arms and tossed it on the bed, then turning her around he held her face in his hands.

"How hungry are you?"

"Extremely, but not for food."

Locking her eyes, he moved his hands to the back of her dress and he slid down the zipper.

"Matt, I feel like I'm dreaming."

"Me too, and I never wanna wake up."

The dress fell from her body, puddling on the thick cream rug under her feet, and in a swift, easy motion, he lifted her up and laid her on the bed.

"Damn, you are gorgeous," he mumbled, removing her black glossy heels. "I've just gotta look at you a minute."

Her long blonde hair splayed around her head, and dressed in only her black lace bra, matching panties, and thigh-high stockings, Matt thought she could be an erotic goddess. Slowly peeling off his shirt, he sat at the foot of the bed and began to softly massage her feet. Closing her eyes, she moaned gratefully as he rubbed and pressed, then rising to his feet, he unbuckled his belt, unzipped his jeans, and stripped down to his underwear. Gazing up at him, she soaked in the sight of muscled torso, his chest dotted with wiry chest hair, and his washboard stomach.

"Please," she begged, raising her arms.

"Try to stop me," he growled, stretching out next to her and pulling her against him. "Uh, Matt?" she whispered urgently, "there's just one problem."

"What?" he asked, his heart skipping.

"I forgot my toothbrush."

CHAPTER TEN

MATT CHUCKLED, KISSED her ferociously, then pulled back and pinned her arms above her head.

"You don't have to worry about the toothbrush," he muttered. "When I stopped to pick up those flowers I bought one just in case."

"Why am I not surprised?" she quipped, grinning up at him.

"A smart cowboy is always prepared."

"What about a smart aleck cowboy?"

"A smart aleck cowboy is always ready to deal with a smart ass cow-girl!" Suddenly clutching her backside and giving it a sharp squeeze, he whisked her panties down her legs. "Damn, girl, you're soaked," he muttered, thrusting his fingers into her pussy.

Moaning loudly, she squirmed against his hand, but leaving her wanting, he trailed his fingertips across her stomach and up to her breasts, quickly noticing her bra clipped in the center.

"Isn't this convenient?" he mumbled huskily, nimbly popping the snap, "or were you hopin' you might get lucky?"

"Aren't you the one getting lucky?"

"Still with the sass," he said with a chuckle, pushing the cups out of the way. "I'll deal with that later. Right now your tits are callin'."

Lowering his lips to her nipples he drew them in, sucking hungrily, evoking soft cries of pleasure. As he released her wrists and slipped off her bra, she threw her arms around his neck, pulled his head down and kissed him fervently.

"You ever been tied up, darlin'?" he muttered, breaking away and staring down at her.

"No, but—uh—"

The edges of his lips curled slightly.

"But you've thought about it."

"I have," she said breathlessly, "a lot."

Lowering his body, he let his weight sink on top of hers and moved his lips to her ear.

"I'm gonna tie your wrists with your bra, and you're gonna keep 'em above your head. You understand me?"

"Yes, yes."

"You're gonna behave, and you're gonna do what I tell you."

"Yes, oh, my gosh, yes."

"Close your eyes and keep them that way."

His body lifted from hers, and she raised her back so he could pull out the sexy lingerie. Wrapping it around her wrists, her thighs tensed of their own accord, but suddenly his tongue lingered on her breasts, moving from nipple to nipple, sucking and nibbling. Surrendering to the sublime attention, she moaned in disappointment as his mouth left her breasts, then gasped as he traveled his lips down her stomach to her soft bush. She held her breath, expecting him to drop his head between her legs.

He made her wait.

Pushing her knees apart, he began kissing the soft flesh of her inner thighs, then feathered his breath over her curly mound.

"Please, Matt. You're driving me crazy."

"Please what?"

"Please stop teasing me, please touch me."

"I am touching you."

"Touch me there," she whimpered. "Please, you're torturing me."

"There? Where is there?"

"My clit. Kiss my clit."

His thumbs gently separated her lips, and dabbing the tip of his tongue against the sensitive knob, he flicked it back and forth eliciting a wail of pleasure.

Dusty was adrift in a sea of sparks. His fingers, his lips, his tongue, sent tingles wherever they landed, and as he devoured her sex, she could feel the promise of a powerful climax. She was wriggling against him, uttering sounds she didn't know she could make, and when he pulled away and rolled her onto her stomach, she prayed he would slide inside her.

Matt stared at her ass. Pink blotches dotted her cheeks, and his eye told him they hadn't all been made when he'd smacked her butt on the patio. Clutching her hips, he pulled her up, and smoothed his palm over her skin.

"Beautiful," he mumbled. "Didn't I promise you a spankin'?"

"No."

"Tsk, tsk. Now I have to add a couple more swats for lyin'."

"No, you don't!"

His response was a series of quick slaps on her right cheek.

"What did you just say?"

"Sorry, sorry," she bleated. "I take it back."

Repeating the rapid-fire smacks on the opposite side, he smiled as the delightful pink stain sprang up under his hand.

"That looks better, but you need more for bein' so dang sassy."

Spanking with an easy rhythm, intending to spark more than smart, he continued until her bottom turned rosy red, then stretching out alongside her, he wiped the hair from the side of her face.

"Hey, baby, look at me."

Her eyelids fluttered open, and she stared up at him with a glazed expression.

"How are you feelin'?"

"Incredible, like I never want this to end."

"Oh, but you do," he murmured, kissing her ear. "I'm gonna roll you over and ride you to the moon, but you've gotta let me know when you're close."

"Uh-huh, but please will you kiss me?"

"Since you asked so nice."

Moving her on her back, he traced his finger around her lips, then dropped his head down and began to leisurely slide his mouth over hers.

Abruptly the kiss became ardent.

A hot flush fired through her body.

She thrust her tongue between his teeth.

Their kiss became a dance, their lips pressing, releasing, sliding and sucking, until he breathlessly pulled away.

"I'm gonna fuck you so hard."

As she let out a strange mewling sound, he reached across to his nightstand to retrieve a condom, then kneeled up and tore open the packet with his teeth. Watching him slide the sheath over his sizable girth, her eyes widened. He caught the gaze.

"Don't worry, I know what I'm doin," he grunted, gripping her hips and pulling her into his pelvis. "Are you ready?"

"Uh-huh."

Placing himself at her slick entrance, he pushed forward slowly, but forcefully.

"Breathe, baby, breathe and surrender," he purred. "Close your eyes and feel me."

His reassuring words echoed through her head, and as he began to thrust, she felt herself open up and accept him.

"There you go, that's it."

His hands tightly grasping her waist, his cock pulled out, then plunged back in, making her gasp, then beg for more. Lifting her pelvis to better his angle, he accelerated, and her single cry became a continuous wail as he rode her forward.

"You close?" he asked breathlessly.

"Yes, yes, yes," she bleated, wishing her hands were free to clutch the rails of the brass headboard. "My whole body is tingling. Please don't stop, I'm begging you, please."

Propelling himself forward, he stroked vigorously, and though his member had been aching to burst, he had managed to hold himself at bay. Now knowing he wasn't going to stop until they reached the pinnacle, he rode her with lustful determination until his release drew near.

Suddenly arching her back, she sucked in a long breath.

"I'm there!" she gasped. "Matt, I'm there!"

Her orgasm took hold.

As her deep, soulful cry filled the room, his groans met her wails, and their shuddering joy consumed them, the spasms shooting tingles through their limbs until utterly drained, they collapsed together, and she melted into his body.

THEY DOZED FOR ENDLESS minutes, then waking from the post-orgasmic bliss, Dusty shifted in his arms.

"Matt, I think I'm getting hungry," she mumbled. "The problem is, I don't want to leave this bed."

"Me too, on both counts," he murmured with a heavy sigh. "Are you okay?"

"Okay? No, not even close. I'm so far beyond okay I don't even think there's a word," she breathed, snuggling against him. "I'm not a leap into bed kind of girl, but it felt right, and it was!"

"Yep, it was. I do have one question though. I don't think I'm the only one who's smacked your butt recently. You wanna tell me about that? I know it's not really my business, but if you have another guy—"

"It's not what you think," she said hastily, interrupting him.

"I'm not thinkin' anything, not yet anyway."

"This is really embarrassing."

"I'm listenin'."

"It was Patrick."

"Say what?" he exclaimed, sitting up and staring down at her. "Patrick? Your trainer?"

"He warned me, but I didn't believe him. It was a first, and it was shocking."

"Why did he spank you?"

"I, uh, did something kind of unethical at the show to another rider. It wasn't cheating exactly, but I, uh, crossed the line. He wanted to make sure I didn't do anything like that at the nationals."

"That sounds like you were a bad girl," he remarked. "A very bad girl."

"I guess. It's just...she's not a very good rider, but she has a ton of money and expensive horses. She ticked me off, and I kind of messed with her head. I couldn't help it."

"Then that spankin' was deserved. You've gotta win fair and square, or it's not a win."

"How can it be fair and square when girls like her have $100,000 horses, and girls like me have to worry about buying a new pair of boots?"

"Do you think she sees it as unfair that you have all the talent? It must drive her crazy to have her daddy's money and she still can't beat you?"

"Huh. I never thought about it like that."

"Gettin' back to Patrick, thanks for tellin' me. I didn't realize you two were so close he felt he could do that."

"He took me under his wing at the barn when I was twelve years old. In a way he rescued me. He's been my best friend, and almost like a second big brother. He really wants me to win, and he doesn't want anything to get in the way."

"Sounds like he's a good guy. Do you wanna be a trainer like him?"

"No, definitely not," she replied vehemently. "You wouldn't believe all the crap he has to put up with. I do want to have my own horse facility though, and do rehab, like I did for Licorice. The property where I found him has so much potential. It's on the market now, not that it matters."

"It is? How do you know?"

"One of the girls at the barn lives nearby. I had to take her home a couple of weeks ago. Anyway, I'm sure I can find a job working at a rehab place somewhere until I can manage to do it myself. Why don't you have a ranch?"

"I'd love to have a ranch, but Silver Streak doesn't give me the time. Runnin' a barn is a full-time job, as I'm sure you know. I'm up here at the lake so I can be near my folks. My dad's not well, and my mom needs me nearby, but I'd really love to roll outta bed and see my horse like you do."

"Oh, my gosh. The answer is simple!" she exclaimed. "You buy a ranch and I'll run it for you."

He paused, then frowned, then smiled.

"You know what, you just might have somethin' there!"

CHAPTER ELEVEN

THE FOLLOWING MORNING Dusty was woken by Matt softly biting her shoulder. His arms were wrapped around her from behind, and sighing a sleepy sigh, she reached back to find his cock already sheathed and standing at attention. As he pushed into her depths, she let out a grateful moan. It wasn't the warmth of his body, or the glorious stroking, or even the joy of waking next to him that sent her into a soft, drifting paradise. It was knowing the torch she had carried in her heart for so many years had finally lit the fire between them.

He tickled her clit and tweaked her nipples, then ravaged her with slow, strong strokes, gradually quickening the pace until they tumbled into a warm, sizzling orgasm.

Drifting in the afterglow, she said a silent prayer of thanks, wondering how she sensed so many years before, Matt Montgomery was the man for her.

"Sure is good to wake up next to you," he murmured, his lips nuzzling her neck.

"It's heaven," she purred rolling over to face him. "Absolute heaven."

"Do you have to work at the show today?"

"Oh, yes, and it will be busy, but I shouldn't call it work. I love it too much."

"You wanna shower here?"

"Yes, please, with you," she sighed, nestling into him.

"I like that idea," he growled, wrapping her in a bear hug, "but it sure is gonna be hard gettin' outta this bed."

"On the count of three?"

"I guess. Here I go. One, two, three!"

She watched him climb off the mattress, then reaching across the bed, he took her hand, helped her up, then led her into the bathroom. It was as unique and comfortable as his bedroom, with brown granite counters, and thick thirsty rugs on top of a flagstone floor. The shower stall had plenty of room to accommodate them both, and she closed her eyes as he soaped her body.

"It's official," she hummed, leaning against him as he moved the cloth down her back.

"What's that?"

"This is the only way to start a morning."

"You won't get any argument from me. It's gonna be almost as hard leavin' this shower as it was gettin' outta that bed."

"Why is Jinxy barking?"

"I usually let him out first thing," Matt replied, handing her the cloth and stepping from the stall. "Dammit. I won't make that mistake again."

"Probably just as well or we might have stayed in here way too long."

"I reckon you're right about that," he said with a chuckle. "Just come on out to the kitchen when you're done."

A short time later they were sharing scrambled eggs, fried tomatoes, toast and coffee, while Jinx panted happily sitting next to Dusty's chair.

"It looks like he wants to be with you more than he wants to be with me," Matt remarked. "Mind you, I can't blame him."

"I think it's because he knows I'll slip him a piece of toast when you're not looking," she said with a wink. "It was probably the secret piece of salmon I slipped him last night that convinced him I'm a soft touch. It was a wonderful dinner, by the way. You're an amazing cook."

"I was inspired," he said softly, then taking a breath, he asked, "When will you be leavin' for the nationals?"

"In about three weeks," she replied, then a frown crossed her brow. "Matt, can I be honest?"

"Sure. Is something wrong?"

"The truth is, I know you'll sponsor me if I'm successful, and that's fantastic, but I'm starting to have second thoughts."

"Really? Don't you want to move into the pro circuit? That's what the sponsorship is all about."

"I know, and I realize there's money to be made. I might consider it for a year, but only to make the bucks. This summer has been fantastic, but do I want to be on the road all the time like my dad? Constantly driving from show to show? I'm not sure it's not for me, and I don't know how it will affect Licorice."

"You sure are competitive for someone who doesn't wanna—"

"Oh, I am," she said hastily, interrupting him. "When I'm racing I want to win, but who wants to be hauling down the freeway every day, and sleeping alone in a motel?"

"You know, Dusty," he said quietly, "I'm real glad to hear that."

"You are?"

"Sure. It's probably a bit selfish, but I'd kinda like to think you'll be stickin' around. Don't worry about the sponsorship thing. That saddle is yours regardless. You deserve it."

"I don't want to let you down."

"Stayin' around here won't be lettin' me down one bit," he assured her, lowering his voice. "You do whatever makes you happy. I'll support you one-hundred percent."

Dusty felt her heart smile, and finishing the last of her coffee, she rose from the table, walked to his chair and pecked him on the cheek.

"Thank you, Matt, very, very much."

"You're very, very welcome."

They quickly cleaned up the dishes, and with Jinx running ahead of them, they made their way into the garage and climbed into the truck, but as Matt backed out on to the road, he suddenly hit the brakes.

"The place where you found Licorice, could you find your way back there?"

"Sure, why?"

"I just wanna drive by it. I'm curious."

"Why do I get the feeling there's something you're not telling me?"

"You said it's for sale and I'm curious," he said evasively. "Point me in the right direction."

"Okay, turn left at the stop sign. It's not far, but go slowly because I'll have to watch for the next street. I only know it by sight and it's easy to miss."

As he accelerated, Dusty stared at him, unable to shake the feeling he was holding something back.

"Quit lookin' at me like that," he said with a grin, glancing at her. "You're makin' me nervous."

"Sorry, but I know something's up. Sorry, you need to turn here," she said quickly as the next street came into view, "then the next road on your left, Cottontail Lane. Take it all the way to the end."

Tall pine trees lined the street, horses grazed in large paddocks, and barns and houses were set back from the road.

"Damn. There are some real nice properties here," Matt remarked. "Why haven't I ever driven through this area?"

"I don't know, but yes, it's lovely up here. The place where I found Licorice is just up ahead, slow down. There it is, the white house with the blue shutters."

"For Sale By Owner. Huh. They're not usin' a realtor, that's kinda weird." Matt remarked. "Where was Licorice when you spotted him?"

"In that paddock by the side of the house. It goes all the way around the back. I guess that's why he was kind of okay. Even though he was by himself, the neighbor's have horses on either side. The girl from

Patrick's barn lives down that dirt road across the street. She said they never see the woman that lives there. She's a total hermit."

"How do they expect to sell this place with no realtor. It's on a dead-end street—no-one will see it—and it's a mess. Look at it. The house is totally run down."

"It was bad when I took Licorice out, but it's even worse now."

"You know, Dusty, it doesn't look like anyone's livin' there," Matt said, squinting as he peered out his window. "Do you see any sign of life?"

"The only thing I see is that old Chevy."

"That car looks like it's been parked there for ages. Look at the dirt on it."

"Maybe it was abandoned along with the house."

"I'm gonna go knock on the door."

"You arc? Why?"

"Why not?" he retorted with a wink. "The land looks decent, and it's surrounded by nice homes. Might be a good investment. Shoot, maybe it even comes with a vehicle!"

"Wow," she said with a giggle, rolling her eyes. "Forgive me for pointing out the obvious, but you run Silver Streak. How will you find the time to oversee a renovation?"

"I'm not even thinkin' about that right now," he replied, turning up the gravel driveway.

Stopping behind the old, filthy, Chevy Malibu, he stepped from the cab and marched up to the front door. Knocking loudly and not getting an answer, he walked around to the side of the house. As he peered into a window, Dusty climbed from the truck and Jinx jumped out after her.

"Should you be doing that?" she asked as she joined him.

"Why not? There's a For Sale sign out front and I'm interested."

"It's creepy here," she muttered. "Like, spooky or something."

Jinx suddenly growled.

Something was wrong.

Slowly turning around, Matt looked towards the back of the house.

A man in dirty, torn overalls wearing a deep scowl on his face, walked towards them. "Whatta you folks want?"

He was tall and thin, with an odd looking mustache.

A chill pricked Dusty's skin.

Jinx snarled, then barked.

Quickly grabbing his collar, she began walking back to the truck.

"I saw the for sale sign and I might be interested," Matt replied casually.

"Oh, yeah? What's your name?"

"Matt."

"Well, uh, come back later, after five. My wife will be here then. She handles all that stuff. Kathy, that's who you wanna speak to."

"Okay, great. Thanks. Do you know how much land there is?"

"A few acres," the man replied vaguely.

"So—room for horses then?"

"Yep, I guess."

"Is there a barn or any outbuildings?"

"Talk to her," the man said gruffly.

"Maybe I could call her? Does she have a number?"

"It's on the sign."

"Ah, right. Okay, thanks for the info."

Jinx was still growling and ignoring Dusty's attempts to pull him to the truck, but as the man turned and marched away, Jinx whined, then finally relented.

But Matt had no desire to turn his back on the scowling stranger and kept his eyes on him until he'd disappeared. When he turned to jog back to the truck, he saw Dusty and Jinx were already safely inside.

"Get us the hell out of here," Dusty said urgently as he climbed behind the wheel.

"You got a pen in that bag of yours?"

"Uh, sure."

"I'm gonna stop at the sign. Write down the number for me," he said as he started backing up.

"Matt, that guy was scary—like—really scary."

"Yep, he was. Something's not right here. Jinx felt it too."

"Does he growl like that very often?"

"Nope, and when he does, he's gotta have a real good reason," Matt replied as he stopped by the sign.

Scribbling the number on a piece of paper and handing it across to him, he stuffed it into his jacket pocket, then drove down the street.

"Was Kathy the name of the woman who had Licorice when you rescued him?"

"It sounds familiar. Yes, I'm sure her name was Kathy. Why?"

"I just wondered."

"Matt, I don't know what's going on at that house, but I do know there's something you're not telling me," Dusty declared. "Be prepared to spill the beans later on."

"Later on? Am I seein' you later on?"

"You are now! When I finish at the show you're going to pick me up and take me to Annie's Eats, then you're going to tell me what the hell this is all about. Maybe you are interested in the property, but there's more to the story, I can feel it."

He was about to protest when he realized there was no point. Dusty had seen right through him, but with any luck the mystery of Black Lightning's legal ownership, and his presence at the ramshackle property, would be solved before he saw her.

"Dusty, I have a better idea. Why don't you and I have dinner again, but at The Sunset Lodge?"

"Wow, two nights in a row!"

"Yep, two nights in a row. Whatta you say?"

"I say, absolutely."

"There's one condition."

"A condition? What's the condition?"

"You bring your hot pink chaps."

CHAPTER TWELVE

WHEN MATT ARRIVED AT Dusty's house to drop her off, he leaned across the console and kissed her, but it wasn't a simple goodbye kiss. It was a long, mouth-to-mouth that he hoped showed her how much he genuinely cared.

"I might call you and make sure you're behavin' yourself," he murmured as he pulled back.

"I can't behave myself all the time. That would be boring."

"Just so long as you remember what will happen if you don't."

"And you, cowboy, have to tell me why you wanted to see the place where I found Licorice."

"You'd better get inside and get ready or Patrick will be spankin' you for bein' late."

"Dammit, Matt! Did you have to bring that up?"

"Gotta keep you on your toes."

Shooting him a look, she climbed out and walked quickly to the front door, then turned and waved as he backed up and drove away. Knowing her mother would have left for work, Dusty made her way to the kitchen and out through the glass sliding door. Hurrying across the backyard to the paddock, she made sure Licorice had been given his morning hay and his water bucket was filled. The goats bleated happily, and Licorice whinnied as she approached.

"Good morning, handsome," she said softly, stroking his neck. "I'll be back to check on you again soon."

The horse nudged her with his head, then returned to his breakfast.

"It's a miracle I found you," she murmured, thinking back to the day she'd come home determined to rescue him. "You never have to worry again. We'll be together forever. I promise."

IF HE WAS GOING TO track down what happened to the champion horse, Matt needed a place to start, and rolling into his parking lot, he prayed Kevin would have news.

When he'd spoken to his father, though he'd never met Black Lightning or his owner, he'd remembered them, and had promised to see what he could dig up. When Matt reached his office, his dad would be his first call of the day.

Climbing from his truck and pushing through the doors, he said a quick hello to Jeanette, then followed Jinx down the hall, into the workroom, and headed directly to Kevin's private studio.

"Ah, mornin', Matt," the master saddle maker said cheerily. "I'm glad you're here."

"Mornin', Kevin. Any news?" Matt asked anxiously.

"I found the file, no problem, but there wasn't much there beyond the basics of the order, but I made a couple of calls and got the low down. John Draper, the guy who used to own Lightnin' lost all his money. I already knew that, but I didn't know what happened to him. Apparently he moved to Miami and he's out of the horse business completely."

"That's good to know. At least he won't want Licorice back, and he should be easy to track down."

"It's not all good news," Kevin said solemnly. "Apparently he put his horses up for sale, but Lightnin' disappeared, and he claimed the horse had been stolen. At the time there was rumor he'd had someone ship the horse outta state and planned to sell him under the radar after the dust settled."

"Why would he do that?"

"Maybe a tax thing, bankruptcy, who knows, but that was the story floatin' around."

"Okay, but if he did, why was Licorice wastin' away in that backyard?"

"Exactly! It makes no sense, and I don't think a guy like Draper would lose track of his horse. I think whoever stole him was forced to dump him, and he spread that rumor as a smoke screen."

"Poor horse," Matt muttered. "So the thief left him with this Kathy woman plannin' to sell him, but ran into a problem. Dusty knockin' on her door must have been a Godsend, but Kevin, what does this mean legally? Is the horse Dusty's, or can a claim be made by John Draper?"

"There's that old sayin', possession is nine-tenths of the law, but you need to talk to an attorney. Regardless of what happened, if he hears about Black Lightnin' and Dusty, Draper could just hop a plane."

"Except he's not into horses anymore," Matt said thoughtfully. "I doubt he'd be bothered."

"That's true, unless he needs the money?"

"Yea, unless he needs the money," Matt repeated. "Thanks, Kevin, I'm gonna call dad and see what his old friends had to say."

"You'll figure this out, Matt, you always do," Kevin said reaching down to pat Jinx.

"From your lips," Matt replied, walking to the door. "If I have to, I'll buy the horse from Draper myself and sign him over to Dusty. I'm not lettin' those two get separated."

Moving quickly up the stairs and into his office, Matt settled behind his desk and picked up the phone. When his father answered full of his usual vim and vigor, Matt found it difficult to believe the man had an iffy ticker. He was always so full of energy.

"Hey son, I've got some information for you."

"Fantastic. Kevin found out quite a bit as well. Let's see how it jives."

"John Draper had a fella working for him by the name of Jim Lewis. He had a reputation as being a moody guy who could be real nasty if crossed. He was tall and wiry and went by the nickname Slim Jim."

"Slim Jim," Matt repeated under his breath, the image of the skinny, scowling man at the run down house flashing to mind.

"When Black Lightnin' disappeared, so did Jim. Apparently the police were lookin' for him to question him about some other investigations, but they couldn't find him."

"So it's likely Slim Jim stole the horse."

"Yep, it's likely, and here's the good news."

"There's good news?"

"I don't know how he did it, but Draper has bounced back in a big way."

"Why is that good news?"

"Seems he's traded horse flesh for horse power. He's heavy into motor racing. He's out of the horse business completely."

"That's what Kevin said, but don't you think that's kinda weird? People into horses have it in their blood."

"You're right, but apparently he was in the horse biz for one reason, and one reason only. Money. Turns out Draper was a horse trader who hired his riders and trainers. I doubt he'd have any interest in Black Lightnin' now."

"That's definitely good news," Matt said, feeling a wave of relief.

"How the horse ended up in that backyard, that's the mystery," his father said solemnly. "It sure is strange. Thank the Lord your friend got him out of there."

"You're not kidding. I went by there this morning, and it's a dump. I'm gonna call our lawyer and get his take, but I'm not worried about Draper. It's obvious this Slim Jim character is behind this whole thing. Thanks, Dad, that's a big help."

"You're welcome, son. My buddies are keepin' their ears to the ground. You let me know if there's any more I can do."

"I will, and I'll keep you posted, pop. Thanks again."

Hanging up the phone, Matt leaned back in his chair and gathered his thoughts. From his father's description, Matt was convinced the lowlife at the run down house was Slim Jim.

"After all this time I can't imagine Draper would have a claim on him, and that creep sure as hell wouldn't."

His cellphone suddenly chimed. Pulling it from his pocket he saw the caller was Patrick.

"Mornin', Patrick."

"Hi, Matt. I'll get right to the point. I found the receipt for Licorice and I discovered something I'd completely forgotten about."

"Good news, I hope."

"I think it is. When I found the receipt everything came back to me. I wanted to make sure the sale would be legal, so I paid the woman $100. Dusty had no idea. She didn't have a nickel back then, and I didn't want her to think she owed me any money. But I had another concern. She was under twenty-one at the time, and I didn't know if she could sign the bill of sale, so I put myself down as the buyer. Of course I'll sell him to Dusty for $1 today, but the receipt spells out everything very clearly, including the description of the horse. Of course it doesn't mean the woman, Kathy Lewis is her name, had the legal right to sell him, but I certainly have proof of the sale."

"Fantastic. That's great. Keep it somewhere safe."

"Of course. Now I have to run. I just wanted to let you know right away."

"I'll talk to you later, Patrick, and thanks."

Matt dropped his phone on his desk.

Kathy Lewis.

Slim Jim's name was Jim Lewis.

There was no doubt about it.

The disheveled, grubby guy at the house was Slim Jim, and he'd stolen Licorice.

"God Bless you Patrick! Now let's see what my lawyer has to say about all this."

THE DAY HAD TURNED hot and sunny. Arriving at the show, Dusty had pulled her hair up under her cowboy hat and donned wide, dark sunglasses. With her light eyes and fair complexion, the sun caused headaches that plagued her during the summer, and she burned easily.

It was nearing lunchtime. Patrick had asked her to work with Amanda Peterson, one of the younger students about to compete in a western pleasure class. The girl's mother was on hand, more of a hindrance than a help, along with several of Amanda's friends.

"Perhaps you could watch over the brood for me, Mrs. Peterson," Dusty suggested. "It's hard to corral them and stay focused on Amanda."

"I'll be happy to," the woman said, and rounding up the excited group, she moved them into the bleachers.

With the mother and children out of the way, Dusty walked into the warm-up ring. Amanda just needed a few helpful hints, and if she applied them, Dusty was confident the girl would be in the ribbons.

Approaching the young student waiting near the gate, Dusty caught sight of a tall, thin, scruffy man wearing a baseball cap. Lifting her glasses, she peered across at him.

Her heart skipped.

It was the menacing man from the property where she'd found Licorice, and he was staring directly at her.

"Dusty? What did you want to tell me?" the young girl asked.

"Sorry, honey," Dusty replied, trying to keep her voice calm. "Think about the rhyme I taught you. Don't perch on your toes, keep your heels down, otherwise you'll look like a clown."

Amanda burst into a fit of giggles. The ditty not only helped the girls to remember, it made them laugh, and laughing relaxed them.

"You're so funny, Dusty."

"Keep that in mind when you go into the show ring," Dusty said, glancing up to see if the man was still there.

She caught her breath.

He had crooked his finger and was beckoning her over.

"Dusty?" Amanda murmured. "Are you okay?"

"Yes, hon," Dusty replied quickly, wondering how the ugly man had tracked her down and why was he there. Regardless, she needed to find out.

"Amanda, walk and trot around for a minute. I'll be right back."

"I'll be fine, Dusty. I know what I'm doing."

"Of course you do, but stay against the rail."

"Okay."

It crossed Dusty's mind to call Matt, but it would take him at least fifteen minutes to arrive, and the man had started walking towards the ring. Determined not to be intimidated, she squared her shoulders and marched out the gate, but as she approached, the lanky man leaned threateningly forward and glowered at her. He reeked of whiskey and cigarettes, and in spite of her resolve, a wave of fear rippled through her body.

"You're the girl who stole my horse."

"I did no such thing," she retorted, her fear suddenly blooming into terror.

"You conned my wife into givin' you my horse, and I'm here to tell you, Miss Champion 1D, Miss Dusty Anderson, Miss Hot Pink Chaps, I'm comin' to your barn and takin' him back. I know you train with that Patrick O'Neal guy, so you tell him to expect me."

"N-no...you can't."

"You bet I can," he snarled, moving his face horribly close to hers, "and I'm warnin' you, give me any shit and I'll rip your long hair outta your scalp, then I'll deal with your boyfriend and that mangy mutt."

"You'll never—"

"I've been away," he barked, cutting her off, "but now I'm back and I've got a buyer ready to pay a shitload, though," he sneered, taking a breath as he blatantly eyeballed her body, "if you're nice to me, and I mean real nice, I just might sell him to you instead."

"He's not your—"

"Yeah, he is, and *my* horse will be stayin' with *me* 'til you and I come to—what you'd call—an agreement. You get my drift? Now listen! I'll be bringin' a rig to your fancy trainer's barn in the next day or two, and *my horse* had better be ready. Don't mess with me, bitch, or you'll be sorry," he finished, then abruptly turned and strode away.

CHAPTER THIRTEEN

FURY AND PANIC BURNING through her body, Dusty summoned every ounce of self-control not to race after the thug and hurl herself at him punching and screaming. Feeling helpless and terrified, she lowered her eyes and clenched her fists as the first tears began to spill. But something made her look up.

The vile man had stopped and was standing just a short distance away.

With an evil smile curling the edges of his thin lips, he raised his arm as if holding a gun, took aim at her head, and pretended to shoot. As she stared at him in horror he broke into a diabolical laugh, then spun around and disappeared across the grounds.

Trembling from head to foot, she dropped to the ground and hugged her knees to her chest.

"Dusty? What's the matter? Who was that man?"

It was Amanda's mother. Grateful the sunglasses hid her tears, Dusty lifted her head.

"It's the sun," she stammered. "It makes me faint."

"But, uh, that homeless man you were speaking with, he seemed to be upsetting you."

"He was. He comes around sometimes. I had to tell him to leave and he wouldn't go," Dusty replied, amazed the lie had come so easily. "I shouldn't have stood in the sun while I was talking to him, but don't worry, I'll be fine."

"I'll take Amanda over to the show ring, shall I?"

"Would you mind? When I've stopped feeling dizzy I'll get under that tree over there. I just need to be in the shade for a few minutes."

"Let me get you there now, and you should have something to drink. I have water in my bag."

With the woman's help, Dusty rose slowly to her feet and walked slowly across to the tall, sprawling oak. Gratefully accepting the bottle of water, she sank into the grass and leaned against the trunk.

"Thanks so much, Mrs. Peterson. I'll be fine. I'm used to this."

"Bless your heart," the woman said sympathetically. "Don't you worry, I'll get the girls over to the ring."

"Thank you. The class doesn't start for at least fifteen minutes. Tell Amanda I'll be there in time."

"You just catch your breath. If you're not it won't be the end of the world."

Waiting until Amanda's mother had walked away, Dusty pulled her phone from her pocket, and with fingers trembling so badly she could barely hit the numbers, she called Matt.

"Please, pick up, please, pick up," she sniffed as she waited.

"Hey hon, how's—"

"Matt, thank God you answered. The creepy guy from the property—he was here. He threatened me. He even pretended to point a gun at me and pull the trigger. He said I stole his horse and I have to turn him over."

"Call your aunt right away," Matt said quickly. "Tell her to send out the security guards. He'll probably be gone, but do it anyway. You can fill me in on the details later."

"Matt —I want to get out of here. I can't stop shaking and I'm worried about Licorice."

"Licorice isn't going anywhere," he said firmly. "I promise I won't let that happen. Now get in touch with your aunt, then get back to me."

"Okay."

Calling Sharon, Dusty relayed the story, then described the menacing, scruffy man.

"Stay under that tree. I'm alerting security right away, and I'll get Jerry over there to stay with you. You know Jerry, don't you?"

"Yes, I've met him."

"Hold on."

As Sharon contacted Jerry Sherman, the head of security, and relayed the thug's description to the guards, Dusty was able to hear every word. It was reassuring, and she found herself calming down.

"All set," Sharon declared, coming back on the line. "I won't have you at the mercy of some crazy loon who thinks he can threaten you like that. Are you going home, or—"

"I wish I could," Dusty groaned, interrupting her, "but I have a girl competing in a pleasure class. I can't let her down."

"Which ring?"

"Ring two."

"Jerry should be there any minute and he'll walk you over. Can you go home after that?"

"I can take a break— but I'll have to come back."

"Let me know when you do and I'll make sure Jerry stays with you."

"Thank you! That would be great."

"Bye, hon. Try not to worry."

"Bye, and thanks again," Dusty replied gratefully, then immediately placed a call to Matt.

"What's happenin'?" he asked urgently. "Are you feelin' any better?"

"I've stopped shaking, so that's a start. Sharon's sent the head of security to watch over me. He should be here any minute."

"Good. Stay on the phone with me until he gets there. When can you take off?"

"I just have one class. The girl is waiting for me now."

"Are you up to it?"

"As long as Jerry is around I'll be fine. Maybe it will help take my mind off what just happened."

"If that bastard ever shows his face again don't engage him. Walk away."

"If I see him again I'll kick him in the balls and stuff them up his ass," she declared angrily.

"Dusty. I mean it. If you see him, get away as fast as you can."

"I'm so scared I'll do that anyway, but you have to tell me what's going on. You knew something this morning. Why didn't you say anything?"

"It was premature, and I know a whole lot more now. Call me when you're ready and I'll come and get you."

"I'd rather just take off the minute I'm done."

"Would you like to meet at Annie's."

"That would be perfect. I'll let you know when I'm on my way. Hang on a second. I see Jerry," she said, feeling a wave of relief as the heavyset man waved at her. "Thank God."

"Make sure he walks you to your car when you leave."

"Absolutely! See you at the cafe."

Ending the call and rising unsteadily to her feet, she gratefully greeted the security chief.

"You can relax. No-one will come near you as long as I'm around," he promised. "You just concentrate on what you have to do. Where are we going?"

"Ring two."

"While we're walking over there, tell me every detail. I want to make a full report. If I ever see the guy I'll be able to hold him and call the police."

They reached the show ring a few minutes before Amanda had to enter. Though Dusty talked to the young girl and gave her some last minute advice, at the forefront of Dusty's mind was the foul-smelling, lecherous man, and his threat to take her precious horse.

OPENING HIS BOTTOM drawer, Matt pulled out a bottle of scotch and downed a quick swig. Dusty's desperate call had unnerved him. Reaching around his chair, he dug into his jacket pocket and retrieved the piece of paper she had handed him that morning. Staring at the phone number, though he wasn't sure why, he decided to call. Picking up his cell phone he nervously tapped in the number and waited. It rang a few times, then what sounded like an old-fashioned answering machine picked up.

"Hello. You've reached Kathy and Jim Lewis. Leave a message."

"My name is Matt, and I'm calling about your house. If you're still looking to sell please call me back."

He left his cellphone number, then ending the call he leaned back in his chair.

"Jim Lewis is Slim Jim," Matt muttered, "but how the hell did he know Dusty has Licorice, and that he could find her at the show grounds?"

A knock broke into his thoughts. Looking up, Jeanette poked her head in the door.

"Sorry, Matt, am I interrupting?"

"Not at all. Come in. What's up?"

"You've made this week's edition of the Gazette," she declared, striding across to his desk and placing the local newspaper in front of him. "Isn't it super?"

He stared down at the photograph. Smiling proudly, Dusty was holding a large trophy and accepting a check from him. Beside her was the big, black, glossy gelding, and above the picture was the headline.

Local girl Dusty Anderson, known for her hot pink chaps, is the winner of Division 1D on her black gelding, Licorice.

"This explains everything."

"I'm sorry, what?" Jeanette asked.

"This article and photograph just solved a mystery. I have to run out for a bit," he said, picking it up. "I won't be long, and I'll be on my cell if you need me. Come on, Jinx. Let's go."

Though Matt knew he'd beat Dusty to the cafe, he wanted to nurse a cup of coffee and think through the complex circumstances before she arrived. The drive was a quick one, and turning his truck into the parking lot, he and Jinx walked to the outside patio. Taking a table under the awning, Mary Jo appeared in a flash, and Matt ordered coffee and a muffin.

"What kind of muffin, Matt?"

"Surprise me."

Sitting back in his chair and idly stroking Jinx's head, Matt thought about Slim Jim's confrontation with Dusty.

"It was kinda stupid puttin' her on notice like that," Matt muttered to himself. "He's probably just after a wad of cash."

"You look deep in thought," Mary Jo remarked, returning with his order.

"I'm trying to decide whether to take the bull by the horns, or let it walk into the china shop and catch it in the act."

"If you let it into the china shop there'll be some breakage," she said thoughtfully, "but if you take it by the horns you might get gouged. Bulls can be unpredictable. I'd tread carefully."

"Mary Jo, you are a very wise young lady," he said with a grin.

"So I've been told," she replied with a wink. "Let me know if you need anything else."

Retrieving the rolled up newspaper from his pocket, he read the entire article as he ate his muffin and drank his coffee, then perused the rest of the local news. Half way through, he heard the click of the gate that led from the parking lot into the patio, and turning around he saw Dusty. Jinx bounded over to her, then running beside and panting happily, he escorted her back to Matt.

"Hi," she said, quickly pecking him on the cheek before sitting down. "I'm so happy to be here."

Her long blond hair spilled around her shoulders, and removing her sunglasses, she dropped them into her bag.

"Excuse me for sayin' this," he murmured, leaning across the table, "but that was one of the sexiest things I've ever seen. I wanna jump on your bones right here, right now."

"I wish you could. That would make me feel so much better."

Reaching to the arm of her chair, he slid it next to his, then put his arm around her shoulders.

"You okay, darlin'?"

"I am now," she said softly, resting her head in the crook of his shoulder, "but will you please tell me what's going on?"

"Yep, and I'll start with this."

Sitting back, he opened the Gazette to the impressive photograph.

"Wow! Mom and Aunt Sharon will be tickled pink, and dad will be blown away."

"Yeah, it's great, but I think this is why that creepy guy was at the show today."

"I don't understand."

"Prepare yourself," he began solemnly. "Licorice used to be a superstar back east. His show name was Black Lightnin'."

"You're kidding? No wonder he's so amazing! But how did he end up here?"

Matt told her everything he'd learned, including how Patrick had found the receipt when they'd picked up the horse, and the comforting assurances his lawyer had given him.

"If you go to the nationals Licorice will probably be recognized," he continued. "That was my biggest concern. I wanted to make sure there was no question of your ownership. Now this creep Jim Lewis has shown up, I'm more worried about what might happen here. The article in the newspaper and the photograph told that jerk who you are, and he came lookin' for you."

"Dammit!"

"Draper has no use for the horse now, and if push came to shove, he'd probably be happy to take a check, but Jim Lewis has stolen the horse once. We could pay him off and he could try to steal him again anyway."

"So what do we do?"

"From what you told me, he thinks Licorice is at Patrick's barn. That's good, but I want to talk about your place for a minute. You have motion lights outside your house, right?"

"Yes, and I can lock the gate. It's hard to see the paddock from the driveway, and Itsy and Bitsy would kick up a racket if someone they didn't know came in the backyard. Dad's coming home tomorrow, thank goodness, so he'll be around, but how do we stop this guy? The police?"

"I thought about that, but he hasn't really done anything criminal—not that we can prove. No-one heard him threaten you, and the ownership of a horse is a civil matter, but I've got an idea or two. Just make sure you're not followed when you leave the show later."

"For sure. I just wish I didn't have to go back."

"One more thing," he said, placing his hand under her chin and tilting her head up. "What were you thinkin', goin' over and talkin' to him?"

"I, uh, wanted to hear what he had to say."

"I should spank you into next Sunday."

"But, there were people everywhere."

"Did that stop him scarin' the crap outta you? Did it stop him threatenin' you?"

"No."

"Don't you ever put yourself in a situation like that again. You walk away and call Patrick or me, understand?"

"Yes, I promise. Um, Matt?"

"Yes, darlin'?"

"I'm so glad you're here."

Seeing fresh tears brimming in her eyes, he wrapped her up in his arms.

"Hey, Licorice will be fine. I've gotta feelin' Jim Lewis is just throwin' mud at the wall and seein' if any of it sticks. A horse is not easy to steal, especially from someone's backyard, and he doesn't even know Licorice is there."

"Thank God," she murmured, sitting back. "Everything you just told me is incredible, but it explains so much. Especially why Licorice is so talented."

"Do you still wanna have dinner tonight? Are you up to it?"

"I do, but now I'm worried about leaving Licorice, although...," she said, thinking for a minute. "I know exactly what to do. Yes, I can definitely join you."

"Great. I'll pick you up at six."

"Wonderful," she said with a smile. "I wish I didn't have to go, but I need to get back." Lifting her head she kissed him softly, loving the warm flush that moved through her body, then stuffing her hair back under her hat, she pulled her sunglasses from her bag and slipped them on.

Watching her walk to the gate, he felt the familiar stirring in his jeans. Shaking his head, he drank the last of his coffee, and dropped his hand to pat Jinx. Gazing idly around the patio, his eyes fell upon the table in the corner. A memory flashed through his head.

"Damn, girl, what happened with you today was like that moment all those years ago," he murmured, "except today I wasn't there to keep you outta trouble."

"It's the first sign of madness," Mary Jo declared as she approached with the coffee pot. "Do you want some more?"

"Yep. I've got some figurin' to do."

"I'm guessing you don't want to break any china, and you don't want to wrestle the bull either," she remarked, topping up his mug.

"That's about the size of it."

"Then you need to let someone else do it for you."

"What did you just say?"

"I said, if you don't want the bull in the china shop, and you don't want to wrestle him yourself, you need to let someone else do it for you."

He stared at her for a minute, then jumped to his feet and kissed her on the cheek.

"Mary Jo, you are the bee's knees!" he exclaimed, and pulling out his wallet he placed a fifty dollar bill on the table. "Keep the change."

"Seriously?"

"Yep, I've gotta make tracks!"

CHAPTER
FOURTEEN

WHEN MATT KNOCKED ON Dusty's door a little before six o'clock, he was welcomed by an unexpected hug from her mother.

"Please come in. Dot is still getting ready," she said as she stepped back. "I've told her father the whole story. How can we ever thank you? Come with me, I have to show you what she's done."

A little taken aback, Matt followed her through the house to the kitchen and out to the patio.

"My genius girl! Look at that," she declared, pointing to the back gate.

A pyramid of empty metal cans rose almost to the top. Matt laughed out loud.

"Clever," he said with a chuckle. "If anyone pushes that gate open it will wake up the whole neighborhood."

"No doubt, and that's the only way into the yard. It's padlocked as well. No-one will be taking Licorice out of here!"

"An intruder could always jump the fence and take them down."

"Dot had the same concern, so she tied them together with some fishing line. If you pull off one, they'll all come down—but this whole thing is just dreadful," she said, suddenly falling solemn. "Dot's just thrilled about her new saddle, even if it is temporary, and she was looking forward to riding over to Patrick's barn tomorrow, but she can't now, not after what that awful man said."

"No, she can't. Being at Patrick's would invite trouble."

"She can go on a trail ride though. She follows a track through the neighbor's field and up a slope. When she's at the top she can look down into the town."

"She mentioned it. Actually, the barn where I keep my horse is at the foot of that hill. I'm hoping to meet her there sometime."

"I'm sure she'd love that. I just hope this nasty business is behind us soon."

"Try not to worry. I have a feelin' it's gonna work out just fine."

"You say that with such confidence. How can you be so sure?"

"Let's just say, I have an iron in the fire," he replied with a wink.

"Do you like my burglar alarm?" Dusty asked, walking up behind them.

"It's brilliant," Matt said enthusiastically. "Where did you get all those cans?"

"Dad likes to refinish furniture when he's home, and they're his empties. He swears he's going to take them to the toxic waste disposal place, but he never gets around to it. I'm really glad about that now."

"Me too," her mother agreed. "I'll never nag him about it again. Now off you go, and enjoy yourselves."

As they walked back through the house, Matt spotted the flowers he had bought Dusty the night before sitting proudly in a golden vase on the living room coffee table. The sight warmed his heart, and as they left the house and walked up to the truck, he leaned in and lightly kissed her.

"What was that for?"

"Just 'cos," he murmured, opening the passenger door. "Let me help you with your bag. Your chaps are in it, right?"

"Uh...no. Why would I bring my chaps?"

A frown crossed his brow.

"Gotcha!" she said with a giggle.

"I know someone who's gonna be gettin' her butt reddened," he whispered, dropping his lips to her ear, then quickly placing the bag behind the seat, he marched around the truck. "Cat got your tongue?" he asked, climbing in behind the wheel.

"I was just thinking about dinner. I'm really looking forward to it."

"Sure, that's exactly what you were thinkin'," he retorted with a chuckle.

"Matt, can I ask you something?"

"Sure. Ask whatever you want."

"Was it my riding that got your attention, or those chaps?"

"Neither," he replied, backing out of the driveway. "It was your flaxen mane flowin' down your back when you were standin' outside Annie's the other day. Mind you, when you started walkin' down the sidewalk, those chaps sealed the deal."

"Flaxen mane!" she said with a giggle. "I love that."

"If I'd seen you all grown up before now I would've been knockin' on your door."

"There's a sign on the wall of Patrick's office, and it says, Mud on my face, dirt in my hair, the way I race, makes the boys stare! It always motivated me. Maybe that's why I thought it was my performance that got your attention."

"You ride like the blazes, no doubt about it, but I felt somethin' that mornin' when I was drivin' by, and it wouldn't have mattered to me if you'd come dead last."

Dusty smiled across at him.

"Really?"

"Really!" he replied, then pausing, he added, "Have I told you how pretty you look?"

"Thank you. You don't look so bad yourself."

"I've reserved us a special table," he said, pulling into the restaurant's parking lot. "We'll be able to see the sun sink behind the hills."

"Matt?"

"Yeah, darlin'?"

"Thank you for everything, especially for looking out for Licorice and me."

Wrapping his fingers around her hand, he brought it to his lips.

"Thank you for lettin' me."

DURING DINNER THEY shared an occasional kiss and sampled each other's meals. Dusty chose apple-raisin cinnamon crumble with ice cream for dessert, and after feeding her the last bite, Matt placed the spoon on the dish and leaned across the table.

"I remembered somethin' today, somethin' that happened at Annie's when you were probably around fifteen."

"Back then I didn't think you even knew I was alive."

"That was just in your head! Anyway, I was with my dad, and you were sittin' by yourself at a table in the corner. A tough lookin' biker walked in and sat opposite you. Do you remember?"

Dusty caught her breath, then silently nodded.

"I couldn't believe my eyes," Matt continued, "and when he left for the men's room—"

"You came over," she said hastily, cutting him off, "and you told me I shouldn't go anywhere with him."

"Do you remember what else I said?"

"A guy like that takes what he wants and I should smarten up."

"Yep, what else."

The memory of the moment flooded her brain. Though she'd been deeply embarrassed, she'd also been thrilled that he'd cared.

"Go on, what else?"

"You said I should have my butt spanked for even having coffee with him."

"Yep, and when he left and you were still sittin' there, what happened?"

"You gave me a thumbs up and paid my bill. When I got home I realized you were right. You saved me that day."

"Dusty, I mentioned that moment for a reason. At the show today, when that jerk called you over, why did you go and talk to him?"

"I know it wasn't the smartest thing I've ever done."

"No, it wasn't. I care about you, Dusty, I care about you a whole lot, and I can't have you takin' chances like that."

"Are you saying you're going to, uh, spank me?"

"Don't you think I should? You knew better, but you did it anyway."

"I guess..." she muttered, searching for something to say that might make him change his mind.

"There's still a part of you that likes to push the envelope just the way you did when you met up with that biker, and that part of you needs to be dealt with."

The waiter arrived and dropped the leather wallet on the table. Matt opened it up, signed his name, and rose from the table. As he took her hand to help her up, butterflies fluttered to life in her stomach, and she felt a rush of warm moisture between her legs.

"Dusty? Are you okay?"

"Yes, fine," she replied, abruptly realizing she wanted his hard hand slapping her backside.

With his arm around her waist they walked out into the parking lot. Though she felt nervous and fearful, she couldn't deny the electric excitement sparkling through her, and the strange desire to be over his knee.

The short drive to Matt's house seemed to take forever.

After Jinx joyfully welcomed them, Matt led her out to the patio. The evening was warm, the moon a cream globe low in the sky, reflected gold on the lake. As she took in the magical view, her eyes caught sight of a double lounger covered with a fur throw. Beside it sat a small table with two bottles of water, along with other items she couldn't quite see.

"Would you like to make love under the stars?" he asked, hugging her from behind.

"I'd love to," she murmured, wondering if he'd changed his mind and wasn't going to spank her after all.

"You can get changed in the bedroom," he whispered, nuzzling her neck. "What will you be wearin' when you come back?"

"My chaps."

"What else?"

"Uh, nothing?"

"That's right, and you've got five minutes. For every second you're late you'll get a swat. I'm already gonna be warmin' your backside, so you might wanna keep your eye on the clock."

Leaning her head against his shoulder, she let out a heavy sigh.

"Matt, you turn me on so much."

"It's mutual, darlin'," he replied softly, then gripping her hair, he tugged it back and locked her eyes. "Now go do as I say."

Though she longed to wrap herself around him and fall on the fur-covered lounger, she settled for a last minute hug before moving inside.

MATT HAD DISCOVERED his love of kink early on. Through his college years he'd enjoyed a number of sexy young women over his lap, and exploring his fantasies with willing girlfriends had been great fun, but being with Dusty was different. His feelings were growing, and a part of him felt slightly out of control.

Peeling off his clothes, he laid them nearby, then lit the hurricane lamp on the patio table. As he stretched out on the soft fur to wait, a rustling sound caught his attention. Turning his head to the sliding glass door, he saw her moving slowly towards him clad only in her hot pink chaps. Her cherry nipples pointed as if begging for attention, and the lamp sent an amber glow against her skin.

"Don't you look a treat. Come over here," he said, checking his watch, then unstrapping it and placing it on the table. "You just made it." Soaking in the sight as she moved across the redwood deck and stood in front of him, he ran his hands over the soft leather covering the inside of her thighs.

"Damn, girl, these are so fuckin' hot."

"I'm glad you like them."

"Dusty, I love 'em."

"They feel really sexy against my skin," she breathed. "I've never worn them like this."

Gliding his palms around her hips, he fondled her naked cheeks, then gripped them as he pressed his lips to her stomach.

"Matt, I feel weak."

Rising to his feet, he wrapped her up, relishing her naked body against his.

"My bad girl," he whispered. "Are you ready for your spankin'?"

"Yes, no, yes."

"I've gotta do it, and I've gotta make it count. You left your young student and confronted a man you were scared of, a man you already thought was dangerous."

"I know."

"I know you know," he said with a sigh, pulling back and staring down at her, "but I've gotta scold you. You need to understand why I'm gonna take a hairbrush to your backside."

"A hairbrush?"

"Yep, just enough to make my point. There's a pillow next to the little table there. I'm gonna sit down, and I want you to put it right where you're standin' and kneel on it facin' away from me."

As she slipped from his arms, he settled on the edge of the lounger, then watched her pick up the cushion, set it directly in front of him, kneel down facing the lake.

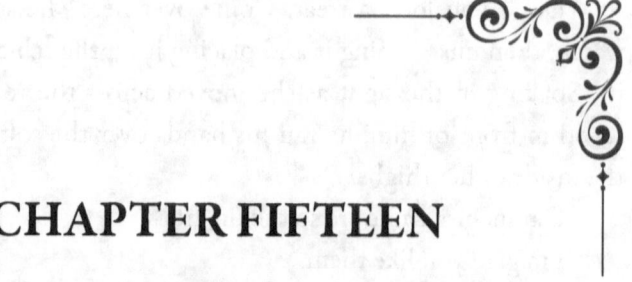

CHAPTER FIFTEEN

AS DUSTY HAD PICKED up the cushion, she'd spotted an oval, wooden hairbrush sitting on the small table, along with a black scarf and two short, leather belts.

"How do you feel, Dusty?" Matt asked softly.

"Nervous, but I'm excited too."

"I'm gonna braid your hair, then you're gonna climb over my knee."

"B-braid my hair?"

"Yep," he replied picking up the brush and moving it through her long, blonde locks. "While I'm doin' that, I want you thinkin' about why I'm gonna make your bottom sting."

"Okay."

"Next time say, yes, Sir," he whispered, pressing his lips against her ear.

"Yes, Sir," she repeated, fresh butterflies bursting to life.

With every tug of her hair, Dusty felt herself sink deeper under Matt's magic spell. Kneeling in only her chaps, her bottom naked and waiting for punishment, though her pulse raced with apprehension, she ached for his touch.

"Couldn't you make love to me now and spank me later?" she begged. "Please?"

He had reached the end of the braid, and was fastening it with an elastic tie.

"No," he said firmly, "and don't ask again. I'm gonna blindfold you. Close your eyes."

His promise elicited a quick gasp, and as the black satin touched the top of her cheekbones, her heart skipped and she gasped again.

"Blindfolds can be scary and excitin' all at the same time," he muttered as he knotted it at the back of her head. "Swizzle around and face me."

His hands gripped her upper arms as she turned, then moved down to her wrists and lifted them up.

"I'm gonna make sure you don't try to interfere when that hairbrush is swattin' your backside."

"I won't, I promise."

"This will make it easier for both of us," he muttered, winding a leather strap around her wrists and buckling it closed, then holding her face between his hands, he moved his lips over hers in a soft, but consuming kiss. "I'm gonna sit back on the lounger, and I want you to crawl over me," he breathed as he pulled back.

"But I can't see anything."

"I'll help you. Stand up and lean over."

Rising to her feet and bending forward, as he guided her over his lap and shifted her into position, she felt the fuzzy blanket under her hands.

"You're at an angle. You can lie all the way down."

As she rested her upper body on the soft cover, he began to caress her upturned cheeks. Sinking into his lap and letting out a sigh, she was almost relaxed, but she knew his sensuous fondling would be short-lived. At any moment she'd learn what it meant to be spanked with a hairbrush.

She'd heard about it.

There had been gossip among the students at the barn. The girls once talked about being swatted by their parents with a hairbrush, but Dusty had never felt such a thing. She'd never been spanked at all until Patrick had done the honors after the episode with Trixie. There'd been nothing sexy about that, not for a minute. The experience had been totally embarrassing, and not one she ever wanted repeated, but being over Matt's lap was something else entirely.

She was tantalized.

Excited.

Scared, but the fear was sultry and salacious.

"Dusty, are you ready?"

"I guess."

"Yes, Sir, or no, Sir."

"Yes, Sir."

MATT GAZED LUSTILY at Dusty's curvaceous globes framed by the hot pink chaps. The sight was even more tantalizing than he'd imagined, and roaming his hand over her cheeks sent a fresh sizzle of energy through his loins.

"You were a very bad girl," he scolded, "and I'm sure this won't be the last time you'll find yourself over my lap. From now on, whenever I have to punish you, you're to present yourself to me wearin' these chaps."

Not giving her a chance to respond, he raised his flattened palm and landed it with a hot sting, and continued to move from cheek to cheek, kissing her backside with fiery slaps. Burying her face in the fur cover, she let out a muffled yelp with each hard smack and squirmed in protest.

"Sir," she yelled, finally lifting her head. "Sir, please, that hurts."

"I'm just warmin' you up," he remarked without pausing his hand. "I told you this has gotta count. You're not gonna be doin' foolish things like that again. I wanna make sure you remember this."

"I will, I will."

"Your butt's turnin' a real nice red," he commented, stopping to study his handwork. "I think you're about ready."

Picking up the hairbrush from the small table, he rested the wooden back on the center of her right cheek and lightly tapped.

"Dusty, this is gonna hurt, and it's meant to hurt. You're bein' taught a long overdue lesson. You understand?"

"Yes, Sir," she panted, "but I promise I won't take any chances like that ever again."

"Uh-huh. That's good, but you're still gettin' you're bottom tanned. Now listen up. Tellin' me it hurts or askin' me to stop is not gonna make a damn bit of difference. I already know how many times I'm gonna swat this hairbrush on your ass. Do we understand each other?"

"Yes, Sir."

"If you've gotta yell, that's fine, just make sure your face is buried in that cover. Here we go!"

Circling the polished wood across her skin for just a moment, he raised it just a few inches, then flicked it down. Though she let out a wail and kicked her feet, he didn't wait for her to settle before repeating the swat on her opposite cheek. She squealed again, but he didn't hesitate, quickly taking it to the sensitive sit spot just above the top of her chaps. Smacking each side several times evoked a howl, but she remembered to bury her face in the fur. Returning the punishment to the center of her bottom, he dispatched several sharp swats before pausing. Gyrating her hips from side to side, she bleated into the lounger.

"Oh, Sir, it hurts so bad."

"Yep, just like I said it would, and I'm almost done, but if I have to spank you for this again," he said sternly, "I'll double the count and make the swats harder. You understand me?"

"Yes, Sir."

"You will not ever," he decreed, landing another hard swat on each cheek eliciting a loud yowl, "put yourself in the company of anyone, man or woman, who could cause you harm in any way. Are we clear?"

"Yes, Sir. Yes!"

"Not in public, or private," he continued, delivering two more, "and no ridin' Licorice where you might be spotted by that lunatic. You get a whiff of danger, you bolt then call me. If you're not sure, you bolt and call me, and when I say you call me, I mean before anyone else. Got it?"

"Yes, Sir, I will, I will."

Placing the brush back on the table, he rubbed her scorched skin until she settled, then slipped his hand between her legs.

"That spankin' sure made you wet."

"I don't know why it made me want you so badly," she mewled, wriggling against his probing fingers.

"Crawl forward and get on your hands and knees."

As she scrabbled from his lap, he kneeled behind her and thrust his fingers into her glistening pussy. Arching her back, she let out a grateful cry and lewdly wiggled her hips.

"Is there something you want?" he teased, shoving his fingers in and out.

"You, your cock, please?"

"Please, what?"

"Please, Sir?"

Grabbing the condom he'd left on the small table, he quickly sheathed himself, placed his turgid member at her entrance, and resting his hands on her hot cheeks, he plunged forward.

"Oh, girl, I'm gonna fuck you hard! I'm gonna fuck you real hard."

DUSTY'S VISIONS OF being gently laid on her back, his mouth softly nibbling her nipples, and his hands tenderly caressing her body, had long since evaporated. She wanted him to ride her roughly and control her, but as he clutched her hips and pummeled her pussy, she found herself swept away by a startling revelation.

She was his to do with as he wished.

The notion evoked a wild cry, and she bucked against him, but rather than respond by quickening his pace or stroking harder, he suddenly slowed. He had sensed her surrender, both her heart and her body.

"Your tits, they're mine now," he growled, reaching beneath her to sharply tweak her nipples and vigorously knead her breasts.

"Yes, Sir," she mewled breathlessly.

"This red ass," he continued, straightening up and landing several hot smacks, "who does it belong to?"

"You, Sir."

"And this wet pussy?"

"Yours, Sir."

Grasping her waist, he began thrusting with strong, powerful strokes.

"You're gonna come for me when I say."

"Yes, Sir...but...I'm there."

He came to an abrupt stop.

"Not until I say."

Her fingers curled into fists.

His control.

She loved it.

Suddenly surging forward, he pumped with abandon.

Her body suddenly stiffened.

The mighty orgasm hovered.

"Come now!" he commanded, tightening his hold around her waist as he pounded. "Right now."

SHE LET OUT A WAIL, but he barely heard it.

Shuddering waves pulsed through his body.

Loud groans bubbled up from deep inside him.

Hot tingles pricked through his limbs, then slowly began to dissipate.

Hearing her soft moans he realized her body had fallen limp. Flaccid and drained, he slipped out and collapsed next to her. Panting heavily, he slid the blindfold from her eyes and unbuckled the leather strap around her wrists, then brought her into his arms.

"Hey, darlin'. Are you doin' okay?"

"Matt," she muttered breathlessly, "I feel something inside me. I don't know how to describe it."

"I know, darlin'. We connected, but we can talk about it later. You just catch your breath."

With her wrapped in his arms on the warm fuzzy blanket, he gazed across the lake at the heavy moon.

Surrender wasn't one-sided.

This wasn't just fun and games.

Dusty had stolen his heart.

CHAPTER SIXTEEN

MATT BLINKED OPEN HIS eyes. When they'd stumbled from the patio and fallen into bed in the early hours of the morning, he'd set his internal alarm clock for 6:30 a.m. It wasn't that he wanted to get up early. On the contrary, lolling in bed with Dusty was a temptation almost impossible to resist, but he'd fallen behind at work and he had to catch up. Disengaging himself from her limbs and rolling on to his side, he found Jinx's face resting on the edge of the bed, his black nose and dark eyes staring at him.

"What's up fella," he whispered, "it's early."

Quickly glancing at the bedside clock he was relieved to see it actually was. Jinx whined, wagged his furry tail, then trotted across to the bedroom door.

Not wanting to wake Dusty, Matt crept from the bed and padded through the house. Jinx trotting ahead of him. Opening the kitchen door, Matt left it ajar, then yawning, he set his coffee pot to brew and decided to shower in the small bedroom off the laundry. There was no reason for Dusty to get up, and using his bathroom would wake her. He'd get some work done in his study, then take her in a cup of coffee when it was time for her to rise and shine.

Standing under the stream of hot water, he thought back to the divine sight of Dusty wandering on to the patio wearing nothing but her hot pink chaps. The erotic image sparked his cock to life, and lathering his hands, with decadent memories of the night before flashing through his mind, he brought himself to a quick and satisfying release. Leaning against the tile wall, he let out a long sigh.

"Dusty Anderson," he muttered under his breath, "you are under my skin big time."

Shaking himself, he stood up and shampooed his thick mop of hair. As his mind cleared, the inspired idea to deal with Slim Jim—compliments of Mary Jo— began to refine itself. If his plan evolved as he hoped, the entire drama with the nefarious horse thief would be over very quickly. There would be no bloodshed, and no danger of Licorice being stolen.

Turning off the faucets and reaching for a towel, he decided to share his idea with Dusty. Not only did she have a right to know what he was about to do, it might help to ease her mind.

Using a bath sheet to dry off, he wrapped it around his waist and headed back to his bedroom to dress. She was still in a deep sleep, and stepping into his closet he donned pressed jeans, a white shirt and light tan boots. Returning quietly to the kitchen, he stood for a moment, trying to figure out what he wanted to eat. Unable to make up his mind, he poked his head out the back door to look for Jinx, but his happy, exuberant dog was nowhere to be seen. Thinking his dog must have come back inside, he closed the door and moved to the cupboard where he kept the cereal. Staring at the boxes, he shook his head.

"No, I don't want cereal!"

"How about some pancakes?"

Startled, he turned around and saw a sleepy Dusty dressed in his robe leaning against the door frame.

"Hey, darlin'. I tried not to wake you," he said, moving across to hug her.

"You didn't, Jinxy did, with a very big, slobbery kiss. It was delightful," she grimaced, scrunching her nose.

"What a naughty dog. The only person allowed to wake you up with a big, slobbery kiss is me. Do you hear that, Jinx, wherever you are?"

The border collie peered around Dusty's legs and stared up at him, guilt written across his face.

"How is it you always seem to know what I'm talkin' about?" Matt asked with a chuckle, "and as for you, Miss Anderson, how is your gorgeous ass this mornin'?"

"About how you'd expect," she muttered, "as I'm sure you probably know."

"So you got the message?"

"Well, duh," she quipped. "You'll never have to worry about me having coffee with a biker again."

"You are such a sassy smartass!"

"I know, but you wouldn't have it any other way. Now, where was I? Oh, yes. I don't cook many things, but I do make outstanding pancakes. Do you have flour and eggs and—"

"I sure do," he grinned, interrupting her. "The pantry is through there."

"Oh, yes, I remember," she said with a yawn, moving out of his arms and ambling across the kitchen. "May I ask why you're up so early?"

"A certain someone has kept me from my work," he remarked, pouring himself some coffee. "I have a stack of catchin' up to do."

"Ah, I see. Then I'd better not take too long making these. Where can I find a bowl?"

"The cabinet to your left," he replied, then walking over to her and lowering his voice, he added, "Dusty, I'm glad you're up. There's something I wanna tell you. Something important."

"Really? Let me guess. You had a dream about being with me on the patio. I was wearing nothing but my hot pink chaps, and you spanked my poor butt with a hairbrush for absolutely no reason at all, then you made mad passionate love to me and stole my heart."

"Good guess, except I spanked your poor butt with a hairbrush because you needed to understand a thing or two," he corrected her, "then I made mad passionate love to you, and *you* stole *my* heart."

She caught her breath.

"I did?" she managed.

"Uh, yeah, you kinda did," he murmured, putting his arms around her waist. "Actually, you kinda have."

Impulsively holding her head between his hands, he gazed at her for a moment, then kissed her fervently, his lips full of the passion and love flowing through his heart. Finally breaking away, he wrapped his fingers around hers and led her to the table, then sat her down and settled next to her.

"I'm not sure how to say this," he began, searching for the right words. "I, uh, I meant what I said just now. I dunno if it's 'cos I've known you for so long, or because we have some kinda natural chemistry, but Dusty, I promise you, you're becomin'...you've become...real special to me. It's happened kinda quick, and maybe that's because of all this trouble about Licorice, but it doesn't matter why it's happened, it has. Are you hearin' me?"

Dusty felt her heart swell, and losing herself in his deep brown eyes, she slowly nodded.

"Matt, I am, and you know I've had a crush on you forever. Obviously I didn't know about the whole control thing, I mean, the discipline thing, and I admit it took me by surprise, but it's weird, I really like it. No, that's not true, I love it and I want it. I'm sitting here with a sore butt, and I really love it. I must be crazy."

"Dusty, if you're crazy, I'm crazy, and I know I'm not. We're a match, but if it ever gets too much you've gotta tell me. Promise me."

"Yes, Matt, I promise," she said earnestly, "but last night—how do I put this? It felt real, as if I was being who I really am. Does that make sense?"

"All the sense in the world," he replied with a smile, "and it makes me real happy."

"Is this what you wanted to talk to me about?"

"Yep, and something else as well. I know what to do about Slim Jim and Licorice. I know how to put an end to it once and for all."

"You're kidding? Really?"

"Yep, and it's clean and it's honest. While you're makin' those pancakes, I'll tell you exactly what I'm plannin' to do, and you can tell Patrick when you see him. Let him know if he has any questions he can call me."

"Fantastic. Tell me. I'm dying to hear."

"Then start crackin' those eggs."

Whipping up the pancake batter, she listened carefully as he relayed his plan, and after pouring them on the hot, buttered griddle, she turned to face him.

"So, what do you think?" he asked, eager to hear her thoughts.

"I can see why Silver Streak Saddlery has become so successful," she said with a grin. "You're right, that will solve the whole thing, assuming it goes as planned. There's one thing that does occur to me though."

"What did I miss'?"

"It's a timing issue. This will take at least a day or two, right?"

"Well, yeah, of course."

"You're assuming it will take Slim Jim that long to get his act together. What if it doesn't? He thinks Licorice is at Patrick's. If he gets a truck and trailer before we're ready, and rolls up to the barn and discovers my horse isn't there, he'll come looking for me. How can we stop that from happening?"

"Dusty, you're right," Matt murmured solemnly.

"There aren't that many haulers in town and I know them all," Dusty said thoughtfully. "Why don't I jump on the phone and alert them that a creepy guy called Jim Lewis might be in touch, and to turn him down?"

"Would they really turn away business for you?"

"Sure. Patrick has his own van, but it's a six horse. We rent the two and three horse trailers all the time. I keep telling him to get a smaller one of his own, but he says it's easier to pick up the phone than deal with another rig."

"That's great, Dusty, and I'll call Rod Clark over at Circus Stables. He has a haulin' service and I know he'll be happy to work with me. Slim Jim will discover Stan's the only game in town. We can control exactly when Jim gets that trailer."

"I wonder if there are any other smaller stables that offer hauling I don't know about."

"I doubt it, but regardless, I'm gonna push and make things happen quick."

"That would be good," she agreed, flipping the pancakes. "Such a drama. Thank goodness I have a super-smart cowboy for a...friend."

She felt her face blush, and cursed herself for her awkward slip of the tongue.

"Hey," he said softly, walking to her side, "boyfriend, partner, you can call me whatever you want. We're an item now, okay?"

As a wave of emotion rippled through her, heat filled the back of her throat, and she turned her eyes up to his.

"I know what you said earlier, but I didn't want to assume..."

"Assume all you want, unless you burn those pancakes, then all bets are off."

CHAPTER
SEVENTEEN

WHEN DUSTY ARRIVED home she was surprised to find her mother busy in the kitchen, humming happily and chopping vegetables.

"Mom, what are you doing here?"

"I called into work and told them I was taking a vacation day. Your father will be home this afternoon and he said he has some big news. I want to be here when he walks in the door, and I'm going to make him his favorite dinner."

"Roast beef with roasted vegetables?"

"That's it, hon. The one that I cook on low and takes forever. These vegetables will be soaking in flavored broth while I run to the market and buy the meat."

"Should I make myself scarce tonight?"

"Sweetheart, would you? I figured you'd probably be off with Matt, but if you don't have plans—"

"It's fine mom," Dusty said quickly. "You can count on having the house to yourself. I have to make some calls before I head off to the show. I hope it'll be a short day so I can ride Licorice up the hill. He needs the exercise, and I can't ride him to Patrick's with that horrible man lurking around."

"I hope you have time too. I think you could use the break, and I'm sure Licorice would love it."

"Fingers crossed," Dusty said, kissing her mother on the cheek. "I wish I could keep you company and chat for a bit, but I have to get moving."

"No problem, honey. You do what you need to do."

Walking swiftly down the hall to her bedroom, Dusty pulled out her cell phone and began calling the haulers she knew. Though she kept the story brief, each of them was appalled someone might attempt to steal Licorice. Her favorite driver, a good-looking young cowboy named Jason, was furious.

"Let him try," he declared "If he shows up I'll turn Baron on him."

Baron was a huge Mastiff, and though he was a gentle giant, he looked as ferocious as a hungry lion.

"How would that work?" she laughed. "Wait, let me guess. You'd hold the guy down while Baron drooled all over him?"

"Ugh. Thanks, Dusty. That's a really gross graphic."

"Yeah, but wouldn't it be great?"

"Hey, I have an idea. We'll catch this guy, tie him spread-eagled to stakes in the ground, pour gravy over his face and let Baron lap it up."

"Oh, my, gosh," Dusty squealed, laughing so hard she had to hold her stomach. "I absolutely love the idea. I can just see it."

"So can I, and Baron's right here. He heard me and he's drooling already."

"I wish I could keep talking, but I have more people to call and I'm due at the show."

"Hey, leave it with me. Things are quiet around here this mornin'. I'll spread the word. Who do you have left."

"You're such a doll. Thanks, Jason, that would be awesome. I owe you one."

"You give me so much business it's the least I can do."

She read him the three names left, then changed clothes and dashed outside to check on Licorice. As she marched across the backyard and entered his paddock, the big, black gelding whinnied his welcome.

"Hey, handsome," she said happily, stroking his neck. "You want some more hay?"

Giving him a little extra and feeding him some carrots, she hurried back to the house.

"Okay, mom, I'm off," she declared, entering the kitchen. "I'll see you later."

"Be careful, hon. Keep your eyes peeled, and if you see that character you steer clear."

"You don't have to worry about that," Dusty assured her, flashing back to Matt's hard hairbrush landing on her backside. "There's no way I'll let that guy anywhere near me."

Heading outside and climbing into her car, she winced—then smiled—as she sat down.

"Say what you will, Matt," she murmured as she headed off to the show. "I must be crazy to like this."

The show grounds were a quick drive, and she called her aunt to let her know she was on the way.

"If that jerk shows up, security will hold him and I'll call the police," Sharon assured her.

"I doubt he'll be back," Dusty remarked. "He probably knows he's a marked man."

"You could be right, and he hasn't been seen, but I'll let Jerry know you'll be here shortly. We can't be too careful. Make sure you keep your eyes open."

"I will. I'm turning into the exhibitors parking lot now," Dusty said, scanning the area for any sign of the villainous Jim Lewis and his battered, old Chevy. "I don't see his car, but he wouldn't be parking here anyway. I need to go. I'm sure Patrick's wondering where I am. Thanks for everything, Aunt Sharon."

"You're welcome, hon."

Pulling into a spot as close to the barn as she could, Dusty locked her car and hurried inside. The show would be over in two days, and grooms were loading trunks and packing equipment. Turning down the barn aisle that was assigned to Patrick's stable, she found a similar scene. Hurrying to the end, she poked her head into Patrick's makeshift office. He was loading up plastic crates.

"You made it," Patrick said as she entered.

"Sorry I'm a bit late."

"No problem, but I'm glad you're here. I spoke to Matt, by the way. He told me everything, including his plan to shut this joker down. He's one smart cowboy."

"Yeah, he is," Dusty agreed, thinking Matt was also the sexiest man on the planet. "But I'm surprised. He asked me to fill you in."

"I called him to see if there was any news."

"Oh, I see."

"I take it you two are an item now."

"We are. Did he tell you that as well?"

"He didn't have to," Patrick replied with a grin, "and I'm very pleased to hear it. I think he'll be good for you."

"Yeah," she said with a sigh. "I have to agree."

"Even though nothing will happen until after the nationals, he's dropping off the sponsorship paperwork this weekend."

"With all the craziness I'd forgotten about that little detail."

"He was going to bring it sooner, but I asked him to wait until the show was over."

"So, where do you need me today? Don't we still have some classes left?"

"Just the team penning tomorrow. Could you finish packing up the office?"

"Sure."

"And I need you to check in with Sharon and make sure everything is up to speed there."

"What else?"

"That's it!"

"This is weird," Dusty muttered, dropping into a chair. "I can't believe it's over already."

"I know. When the show comes to an end, it seems to happen suddenly. I don't quite understand it. I never have."

"The nationals are around the corner," she murmured, a frown creasing her forehead. "I sure hope Matt's idea works."

"It will. Keep the faith."

"I still can't believe this whole thing with Licorice has happened."

"It's not what life throws at you that matters, it's how you deal with it," Patrick said solemnly, "and it seems to me Matt has it well in hand. I have to run. Try not to fret. I'm sure it's all going to work out."

"Patrick?"

"Yes, Dusty?"

"Thank you for everything you've done for me," she began, an unexpected swell of emotion welling up inside her. "I don't know what my life would have been like if you hadn't taken me into your barn. I know I wasn't easy, especially at the start."

"Hey, where is this coming from?" he asked, sitting in the chair next to her.

"I don't know. Maybe it's because of what's happened with Licorice and that horrible man, or maybe finally getting together with Matt after all these years. Don't get me wrong, it's amazing, but it's also kind of overwhelming. I guess..." she said, taking a breath and looking at him. "I just wanted you to know how important you are, and how much I love you."

"Dusty," he murmured, putting his arm around her shoulders, "you're like the little sister I never had. I love you too, and I'm very proud of you."

"I know I do stupid things sometimes," she sniffled, a stray tear trickling down her cheek, "but I do try."

"Of course you do. Trust me, there are days I don't know what I'd do without you, and it's okay to feel a bit emotional right now. You've been dealing with so much. You still are."

"It has been a bit crazy," she murmured, taking a deep breath, "but I'm fine now. Really."

"Are you sure?"

"Yes, I'm sure," she replied, nodding her head. "Honestly."

"Finish up here, check in with Sharon, then you can take off."

"I can?"

"You bet. You've worked your ass off this show, and the girls will all pitch in."

"Thanks, Patrick. I am a bit tired today."

"I know," he quipped with a grin, "but I won't ask why!"

His comment made her smile.

Kissing her on the forehead, he marched away, and she let out a weary sigh.

"Man I'm beat," she mumbled, "but I have to take Licorice out on the trail when I get home. We both need it."

"Dusty?"

Jumping to her feet and turning around, she found Jerry standing in the door.

"Sorry, I didn't meant to scare you."

"That's okay. I was just thinking about stuff."

"I'm your official bodyguard again, and happy to do it."

"Great. I won't be here long, but I'm very glad to see you."

SITTING BEHIND HIS desk in his office, Matt leaned back in his chair and smiled broadly. He had just set his plan into action and things were going well. Picking up his cellphone, he placed a call to Rod Clark, the manager at Circus Farms.

"Hey, Matt, how are you?" Rod asked as he answered. "Jackson's been wondering where you are."

"Give him an extra carrot and tell him I'll see him soon."

"Sure will. What can I do for you?"

"A guy called Jim Lewis will be calling you, and I have a very big favor to ask."

Rod listened carefully, and quickly agreed to Matt's request.

"Thanks so much for this, Rod. I owe you one."

"Hey, I'm happy to help. Scumbags like him need puttin' away. Horse thieves are the lowest of the low!"

"Yeah, they are, especially this one. I'll speak to you soon."

Ending the call, Matt felt a flood of relief.

"Well, Jinx," he murmured to his dog lying next to his chair," it looks like things are under control. Time to get back to the business of Silver Streak for a while."

IN THE WHITE SHABBY house with the blue shutters on Cottontail Lane, Slim Jim was lying on a torn couch watching a horse race on television, and drinking Three Ships whiskey from a bottle.

The black wooden coffee table was strewn with ashtrays waiting to be emptied, and the remnants of several burger takeaway meals. In the midst of the mess was the Gazette, open to the page showing the photograph of Dusty Anderson, her black gelding, and Matthew Montgomery.

Initially Slim Jim thought he'd scare five grand out of the kid that had taken the horse, then suddenly everything changed.

"Idiot," he muttered, downing another swallow of the cheap liquor and staring at Matt's image in the newspaper. "If you hadn't shown up here, I'd never have known you were friends with that blond. That was so fuckin' stupid," he drawled in his half-drunken state. "Twenty-five grand should about do it, but I sure would like to get me some of that blonde pussy. Fuck. With that kinda money I can get all the blonde pussy I want. I guess it's time I rented me a trailer. Where's that fuckin' phone?"

CHAPTER EIGHTEEN

FINISHING UP AT THE show took longer than Dusty had thought it would, but not because of work. The young girls wanted to chat, and friends who lived in a neighboring county needed to say their farewells. By the time she returned home it was almost one-o'clock, and her mother was busy cleaning the house.

"I was going to take Licorice for a trail ride, but if you need help I'll be happy to stay," Dusty offered. "I don't mind."

"No, no," her mother replied with a happy smile as she bustled about. "You take off. I'm doing this more because I want to than I have to. I just seem to be filled with energy."

"It's so good to see you this happy."

"Your father's coming home, and that always makes me happy. It's not easy being married to a man that's on the road so much, but when he walks through that door, it's worth it."

"I've been a bit distracted with everything that's going on, but I can't wait to see him," Dusty said, suddenly realizing she didn't want to become a rodeo pro and live half her life on the road.

"You go and get on that horse of yours. He's been out there standing at the fence waiting for you. It's almost as if he knows what's coming."

"I told him before I left. I swear he speaks English. I'm going right now."

Heading to her bedroom and changing into her favorite riding jeans, she opened her bag to pull out her chaps. Just the sight of them made her tummy tumble. Pausing, she closed her eyes and relished pleasure of the moment.

"I can't wait to see you again, Matt," she murmured, then buckling them at the waist, she slid the zipper down the sides of the legs.

Leaving the house, she hurried out to the paddock, stopping to pet Licorice before entering the small shed that served as her tack room. Removing the cover from the Silver Streak saddle, she gazed at the rich leather and fine craftsmanship.

"I can't believe I'm going to own one of these," she muttered happily. "All those years of sweeping and cleaning and exercising other people's horses is finally paying off."

Picking up a halter, she wandered into the paddock. Licorice immediately ambled over to her, gratefully accepting the carrot she offered.

"You're such a good boy," she said with a sigh. "You and I are so lucky to have found each other."

Leading him to the hitching post, she brushed him off, cleaned out his feet, then tacked him up, making sure she had everything she might need. Her phone was safely zipped into her jacket pocket, and a saddlebag held binoculars, water, a hoof pick, and a few granola bars. Finally set, she slipped on his bridle, led him to the mounting block, and climbed on board.

The heat wave had lasted only twenty-four hours, and a cool breeze wafted around them, but Dusty barely noticed the weather. She was elated to be off on a ride, and though the saddle was exceptionally comfortable, her backside was still a bit tender. The memory of her decadent night sent a smile across her lips.

There were only two gates to open and close before starting up the hill, and though thrilled to be out on the trail and full of pep, Licorice remained a perfect gentleman each time she had to dismount and climb back on board.

The path was wide and well used, the footing safe and soft. When Dusty asked Licorice to move into the canter, he tossed his head and sprinted up the gentle stope. Reaching the top, Dusty gazed across at the busy town below, then decided to ride down to Circus Farms at the base of the hill to meet Jackson. She was about halfway down when Matt's warning words echoed through her head.

No ridin' Licorice where you might be spotted by that lunatic.

"Shit," she exclaimed, bringing her horse to an abrupt halt. "It would be just my luck to be ambling around down there and have that maniac show up."

Sighing, she started back up the hill, but when she reached the top and turned around for one last look, her eyes grew wide. An old, battered car was driving into the parking lot. Grabbing the binoculars from her saddle bag, she peered down at the tall, thin man as he climbed out and strode towards the office.

"Holy crap! It's him," she muttered. "Thank God I came back."

Quickly returning the binoculars to the bag and retrieving her phone, she called Matt.

"Hey, darlin'. What's up?"

"I'm sitting on Licorice at the top of the hill looking down at Circus Farms, and Slim Jim just drove up. He's in the office now," she said anxiously. "Were you able to reach the manager?"

"Yep, I reached him, and it's all under control."

"My heart is pounding so hard I swear it's going to jump out of my chest. Just seeing him is making me panicky."

"Take a deep breath," he said calmly. "It's all good, darlin', I promise."

"I'm so glad I was able to reach you. That was a close call, but hearing your voice is calming me down."

"Hearin' yours is havin' the opposite effect on me," he said with a chuckle.

His comment evoked a giggle.

"You're incorrigible."

"I hope so."

"Matt," she began hesitantly, "can I ask a favor?"

"Sure."

"Dad is coming home and I told mom she could have the house to herself tonight. Can we get together?"

"You bet. Why don't you come over here later this afternoon? I need to show you some leather samples, and we can have a bite to eat in town."

"That's sounds perfect. What time?"

"Everyone leaves this place at five-thirty, so any time around then. Call me when you pull into the parking lot and I'll meet you."

"Wonderful. Hey, Matt—he's leaving," she remarked, seeing Slim Jim walking back to his car.

"Dusty, what did you mean when you said you had a close call?"

"Uh, nothing. I'll tell you later," she said evasively. "I should proba-bly head home."

"You do that, and ride safe."

"I will. Bye."

Ending the call, she rolled her eyes.

"Me and my big mouth," she mumbled, slipping the phone into her jacket pocket and zipping it up. "He'll ask me again, I know he will."

Moving down the gentle slope, she broke into a canter across the field, and as the house came into view, to her great joy she spotted her father in the backyard. She was about to call out to him when he sud-denly spun around, waved, then broke into a jog, leaping over the first gate and sprinting to the second.

"Hey, honey," he said excitedly, opening it as she approached.

"Hey, dad! It's so good to see you."

"I'm so proud of you!"

Jumping from the saddle, Dusty hugged him tightly. In spite of the long hours on the road Tom Anderson had kept himself in shape. He was a big man, tall and broad, and she let out a squeal as he effortlessly lifted her into the air just as he had when she was little.

"My champion," he declared, setting her back on her feet, "and your mom tells me you're in love. We've got some celebrating to do."

"She did? Damn! Can't a girl have any secrets?"

"Not in this family," he said with a chuckle. "Let me give you a leg up."

As they made their way back to the house, he asked how she'd met Matt, quizzed her with endless questions about her encounter with Slim Jim at the show grounds, then wanted to know the details of Matt's plan.

"Sounds like he has a solid strategy, but, Dusty, you shouldn't have spoken to that Slim Jim character. He's obviously dangerous."

"I know," she muttered. "It was stupid. Matt was upset with me too."

"Don't go putting yourself in a situation like that again!"

"Good grief, you and Matt! You don't have to worry. I won't."

Reaching Licorice's paddock, as Dusty climbed down, her father let out a low whistle.

"That's one heck of a saddle!"

"I know! Isn't it gorgeous? It's amazingly light, and so comfortable."

"Seems like this guy is doing right by you. He'd better. Get finished and come into the house. I have some news."

"Can't you tell me now?".

"No, I'm telling you in the house. I love you kitten," he said with a happy grin, then hugging her again, he marched away.

"He and Matt are bookends," she declared, looking up at Licorice. "At least you can't boss me around."

The horse suddenly shoved her with his head.

"What the hell?"

He shoved her again.

"Okay, okay, I'll get you a carrot," she said impatiently, then realizing what just happened, she burst out laughing. "Yeah, well, there is that."

Quickly putting away her tack and brushing him off, she hurried back to the house. Entering the kitchen, she found her parents at the table drinking a bottle of champagne, and a full glass waiting for her.

"What's all this?"

"First, to celebrate your win," her father said proudly. "Second, my promotion."

"Will you be driving a bigger truck," she asked as she sat down, "or routes closer to home?"

"Neither. They're opening a depot right here in town, and I've been given a management position. No more long hauls."

"What? Dad, that's absolutely fantastic," she exclaimed, jumping up and hugging him. "How did this happen? When did this happen?"

"I was interviewed before I went out on this last run, but I didn't mention anything about it because I didn't want to get anyone's hopes up. Anyway, I had some ideas and I mentioned them in my interview, and I guess the bosses liked them. I'll be involved in getting everything set up, then I'll have a hand in running things."

"Dad, I'm so happy for you," she exclaimed, tears in her eyes. "I'm so happy for us!"

"Me too, honey. They're giving me a week off to catch my breath, and the money, it's way better!"

"Dad, you deserve every single penny, and the break," she declared, sitting back down, then looking across at her mother, she realized she hadn't said anything. "Mom, are you okay? You're so quiet."

"I've just been hoping for a day like this for so long, and now that it's here, I'm just... " but her voice drifted off as the emotion took hold.

Sliding his chair closer to his wife, Tom Anderson put an arm around her and joked about how she'd soon be sick of the sight of him.

"Never," she sniffled, "not in a millions years."

Dusty felt a warm shiver ripple through her body.

Matt owned Silver Streak Saddlery and lived in a lovely home overlooking the lake, but she didn't care. She loved the man he was, and how she felt when she was with him.

What did you mean when you said you had a close call?

His question flashed through her mind.

Her butterflies suddenly burst to life.

"Now we just have to get through this mess with Licorice," her father declared, breaking into her thoughts. "We'll drink our toast, then talk about Matt's plan. I want to help. It wouldn't be right if I didn't."

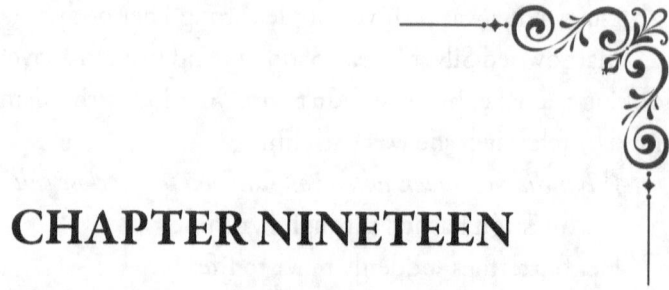

CHAPTER NINETEEN

IT WAS A FEW MINUTES after closing time at Silver Streak saddlery. All the employees had left, and moving through the large work space with Jinx trotting along at his side, Matt headed to the reception area to wait for Dusty.

He was fastidious about the work space. At the end of every day, he'd pick up any bits of leather left on the floor, or any garbage spilling out of waste bins. Though cleaners came regularly, they weren't allowed in the workroom. That was cleaned by two of the junior staff.

Pushing through the heavy steel door, he walked down the wide hallway and into the reception area, but glancing out the window into the parking lot, panic sliced through his heart.

Dusty was leaning back against her car with Slim Jim towering over her.

His first reaction was to bolt through the door, grab the man, hurl him to the ground and beat the crap out of him, but he paused.

"He's gotta know I'd see him," Matt muttered under his breath, his heart pounding as his mind raced. "If I punch his lights out I could be the one in handcuffs. Shit, this is one smart guy."

But Jinx had sensed something, and was already bounding to the front door barking and snarling. As Slim Jim spun around at the noise, Dusty ducked away and bolted the short distance to the building. Managing to grab Jinx by the collar as he opened the door, Matt held it as she darted inside.

"Hey, dickhead," Slim Jim shouted before Matt could close the door. "Twenty-five grand in cash, tomorrow, four-o'clock at O'Neal stables. I'll be there with a truck and trailer. No money, I'll take the horse, and if anyone tries to stop me there'll be trouble, big trouble."

Jinx was still snarling and barking, and realizing Matt was barely able to hold him and the door, Dusty hurriedly slipped her hand through his collar.

"I've got him, Matt, I've got him," she said urgently, pulling Jinx away.

"You'll have your money," Matt called, straightening up, "but if you come near Dusty or show up at Patrick's barn before then, you're the one who will have big trouble."

"Just make sure you bring the fucking money, and I mean cash," Slim Jim scowled, "or that girl of yours will be real sorry."

"You come near my horse and I'll blow your fucking brains out," Dusty screamed, still holding Jinx and shouting from behind Matt.

"Okay, Dusty, okay," Matt said hastily.

"I mean it! I'll get my dad's shotgun and blow your fucking brains out!"

"That's a real spitfire you've got on your hands," Slim Jim yelled back. "I'd sure like to get me some of that. Is she a whiner or a screamer?"

"You're an idiot, Lewis. You think I'm gonna fall for that old trick? You think I'm gonna lose my temper and come at you? You're outta your mind. This is private property, you're trespassin' and I'm callin' the police right now."

"Glad you mentioned the police," Slim Jim shot back. "One word to them and that girl of yours will arrive at the barn one day and find her horse either gone or dead, and I'll be miles away. You got me? Not one fuckin' word. I keep my promises. Screw this up, and she gets screwed, and when I say screwed, I'm not just talkin' about her horse."

Wanting the drama to end, Matt slammed the door shut and locked the bolt. As Slim Jim jumped in his car and peeled out of the parking lot, Matt turned to Dusty. Her face was white, her eyes wide.

"Matt...?"

"Dusty," he said calmly, stepping towards her, "you can let Jinx go now."

"Oh, yeah."

Pulling her into his arms as she released Jinx, he could feel her trembling.

"Come and sit down. Tell me what happened. Did he follow you here?"

"I have no idea," she murmured as they settled into a couch against the wall. "I drove into the lot, got out of my car, and he was just standing there, but I wasn't really paying attention. When I parked I looked down to pick up my bag. I guess he must have driven in right at the moment."

"I have a feelin' he was watchin' this place, or maybe watchin' me. He was probably parked on the street, and when you drove in he grabbed the opportunity.

"You think?"

"I've gotta admit, he's smarter than I gave him credit for. What did he say to you?"

"He said if you didn't show up at Patrick's barn tomorrow at four o'clock with twenty-five grand in cash, he'd take Licorice and I'd never see him again. He said he already had a buyer lined up in another state. Then...uh...he said some other stuff."

"Did he threaten you?"

"He was starting to when Jinxy barked."

"Figures. He wanted to goad me into doin' something stupid. Are you okay?"

"I feel all trembly. I'm so glad my dad is home."

"He's back?"

"Yes, and I'm so glad," she repeated.

"How about we go up to my office and have a drink?"

"That sounds good. Sorry I started yelling at him. I couldn't help myself."

"That's how creeps like him operate. They try to provoke you, and if they can get you to react badly it gives them the upper hand. If I'd jumped on him, which believe me I wanted to do, I could have easily wound up in the back of a police car."

"I don't understand. He was threatening me. You would have been coming to my rescue."

"Yep, but he didn't lay a finger on you. There are security cameras lookin' down on the parkin' lot, and whatever happened would have been caught on tape. The guy who throws the first punch is the guy that gets hauled away."

"Oh, Matt! You were so smart to think of that."

"Come on, let's get that drink."

Taking her hand, he led her down the hallway and through the heavy steel door, but as they headed across the expansive workroom, Dusty spied the saddle on display. Her fantasy suddenly flashed through her mind. In spite of the frightening episode she felt a flutter in her stomach.

"Matt?"

"Yes, darlin'?"

"Can I look at this saddle for a second?"

"Sure. Do you like it?"

"I do, but the thing is..."

"The thing is what?" he asked, puzzled by her expression.

"Believe it or not, I had a very naughty dream about your workroom just like this, and, um, a saddle on display just like this."

"I see," he murmured, wrapping her up. "Do you wanna make that dream come true?"

"Uh-huh," she breathed, a blush crossing her face.

"Bringing your fantasy to life would be my very great pleasure, but first, I need that drink."

"I do too."

With Jinx leading the way, they climbed the stairs and entered his office. Dusty dropped on the sofa while Matt opened a locked cabinet behind his desk.

"I have, beer, brandy, wine, scotch, or vodka."

"Vodka. A shot would be perfect. Why do you have such a well stocked bar?"

"I have visitors. They come in, I take them on a tour, then end up here in my office. I get them a bit buzzed and they place an order," he replied with a grin. "Or they place an order and we celebrate."

"Women too?"

"I'm not gonna lie to you. Yeah, there have been a couple."

"Have you ever done anything with a woman in the workroom?"

"No, Dusty, I haven't," he said patiently, moving across the room and handing her the glass. "On to another subject. What did you mean today when you said you had a close call?"

"I plead the fifth," she retorted, then downed the shot of vodka. "Thank you! I needed that."

"Pleading the fifth doesn't hold water with me. Do you want another?"

"I think so, yes, please."

Fetching the bottle and carrying it back to the couch, he poured in a second shot, then stood over her while she drank it.

"Out with it. Tell me what almost happened."

"It was nothing!"

"Nothin', huh," he murmured, returning to the cabinet. "Let me guess," he continued, grabbing a glass and splashing in some whiskey. "You were ridin' down the hill to Circus Farms when you saw Jim's car drive in, so you turned around and hightailed it back up the hill."

"Not exactly," she replied as he ambled back to her. "I did start riding down, but I remembered what you said about not going anywhere I might run into him. That's when I turned around and went back up the hill. I didn't see him until I'd reached the top again. He was pulling in, and I called you."

"So—you remembered my warning, but only after you'd already started down the hill."

"Yes, but I did remember! And I didn't keep going after I did."

"Hmmm, muddy waters," he muttered with a frown.

"That vodka is kicking in already. What a day. I haven't had a chance to tell you the fabulous news. My dad has been promoted. The company's opening a depot here, and he's going to help start it up, then manage it. He's not going back on the road. Mom is so happy. They both are."

"That's rare, a driver breakin' through like that."

"Dad's a smart guy, but he didn't go to college. That's why he was so determined that Rob and I get an education. He's talented too, with his hands. He can figure things out and make things work."

"I'm lookin' forward to meetin' him," Matt said with a smile, "but right now I'd like to spend some quality time downstairs with his daughter, bent over a certain saddle."

As a wave of excitement sent her butterflies to life, she swung her legs over his thighs and curled against his chest. Placing his glass on the side table, he clutched a fistful of hair, tilted her head back, and dropped his lips to her neck.

"Ooh, Matt, that makes me crazy."

"Uh-huh," he murmured, moving his mouth to the hollow of her neck.

Quickly popping the buttons of her pink and white checked shirt, he pushed the fabric apart and gazed at her naked breasts.

"No bra? What a welcome surprise," he muttered, lowering his lips to mouth her nipples.

Continuing to hold her hair, he devoured her breasts, his free hand holding them as he sucked, nibbled and tongued. When she split her legs and arched her back, he released her hair and sat up.

"I think it's time to take this downstairs."

But before she could slip off his lap, he suddenly sank his lips against hers, devouring her mouth in an endless, fervent kiss.

"I'll be back in a second," he whispered, "and when I return I expect you to be naked except for your panties."

CHAPTER TWENTY

DUSTY HAD JUST REMOVED the last of her clothing when Matt returned wearing a terry cloth robe and carrying another over his arm.

"Where did those come from," Dusty asked, "and why do you have two of them?"

"I built a small workout room with a shower when I first took over for dad. I was puttin' in such long hours I couldn't get to the gym. Put this on," he replied with a grin, handing her the extra robe. "Jeanette thought I needed a new one. It was a Christmas present. I just never took the other one home."

"A likely story!"

"Come on, sassy girl," he grinned, pulling her to her feet and swatting her butt. "Your saddle awaits, and Jinx, you stay here and guard the office."

Closing the door behind them, he took her hand as they started down to the workroom.

"Why did you leave Jinx in your office?"

"If there are leather scraps around he eats them. Don't ask me why."

"Oh, like a puppy tearing up shoes."

"Something like that I guess."

They'd reached the bottom of the stairs, and grabbing her around the waist, he jerked her into his body.

"You might be getting a bit more than you bargained for."

"What do you mean?"

"You'll find out, but if it's too much just say red. Red means stop, but only say it if you mean it."

Her heart jumped.

"Matt, you've made me weak again."

Swiftly lifting her off her feet, he carried her across to the display, stood her in front of it and slid off her robe, draping it over the saddle.

"Spread your legs and lean over the saddle."

Her fantasy was becoming a reality, and with her pulse racing she bent forward. A moment later he had wrapped a cord around each of her ankles, tying them to the display stand. She suddenly felt lewdly exposed.

"First, we're gonna have a reminder lesson," he declared. "It's good you saw sense, but halfway down that hill was halfway too far. You understand?"

"Yes, Sir, I understand."

"This may be the first time you're over this saddle, but you can bet your beautiful backside it won't be the last. I like you this way, I like it a lot."

Her thighs tensed, with a shudder of need rippling through her sex, she softly whimpered.

"What is it?" he asked, playing with the elastic of her panties.

"I'm just so turned on."

"You sure are," he mumbled, sliding his finger inside the gusset and tickling her clit.

Closing her eyes, she moaned softly, then gasped in shock as he suddenly yanked her panties into the cleft of her cheeks.

"This is a yardstick," he murmured, grabbing it from a nearby bench and gliding it across the center of her backside. "I can't let you go unpunished. You were right, it was a close call, much too close."

"At least I turned around and went back."

"Yep, at least you turned around and went back, and if you hadn't you'd be in a mess of trouble."

He'd deliver just enough to let her know her sins would not be left unpunished. The ruler was thin and light, but when he'd tested it on his thigh he'd found it carried a sharp sting.

"Three quick licks on each cheek, and we'll say no more about it."

Dispatching the first triple on her right globe, he was delighted to see the inch-wide, red stripes bloom to life. She gasped and squirmed, but didn't cry out. Moving to her opposite side he repeated the discipline, evoking a loud yelp.

"I hope that was enough to get my point across."

"It was, Sir, definitely."

Moving back to the workbench, he put down the stick and picked up a short, thin knife, quickly returning to slice through the sides of her panties. She let out a cry, but didn't move. Leaving them dangling and held in place by her hips against the saddle, he lowered the remaining fabric nestled in her cheeks, letting it drop between her legs.

"Very sexy," he muttered, stepping back and enjoying the sight.

As she wriggled in response, he grabbed the condom he'd slipped in his pocket, sheathed his rigid cock, and touched it against her pussy.

"Do you want this," he whispered, leaning over her and placing his lips at her ear. "If you do, ask nicely."

"Please, Sir, may I have your cock?"

"I'm not sure," he teased, slightly pushing in a short distance then pulling way. "That didn't sound very urgent. Try again."

"I want you!" she exclaimed. "Is that urgent enough?"

"It was, but not very polite."

"Oh, Sir, please will you fuck me?"

"In a few minutes. I don't think you're quite ready."

"But I am!"

"Nope. Your kitty needs some discipline."

"What?"

"I said your kitty needs some discipline," he repeated, cupping her sex and squeezing.

As he moved his hand back, he heard her take in a breath. He paused, then landed his palm down with a soft slap. Before she could mutter a complaint or bleat out a moan, he spanked again, then again, landing a flurry of light, tantalizing smacks.

"Let's see if it's behaving itself now."

"Ooh, Sir...please..."

"The only problem havin' you over this saddle," he remarked, driving a finger in and out of her hot depths and rubbing her clit with his thumb. "I can't get to your tits. I'm gonna have to make up for that. One night real soon, I'll spend an hour with each of them."

As his promise delivered a fresh tide of moisture through her saturated sex, he broke into a grin, placed his cock at her entrance and thrust forward.

BEING STRETCHED OVER the saddle with her legs spread and bound, and the soft robe offering unexpected comfort, Dusty found the reality far more electrifying than her fantasy. His cock pounded her pussy, and her decadent exposure fueled the erotic fire surging through her body. She suddenly cried out in shock.

A slippery visitor pressed against her forbidden back hole. She wanted to scream out, *red*, but as the unwanted intruder insisted she allow its entry, his cock continued to ravage her and she could feel her climax building. Though she was mortified, she didn't want to stop the onset of her powerful orgasm.

"Behave," he growled, landing a hot smack. "Accept it! Now!"

Compelled to obey his command, the interloper slid inside.

Her climax abruptly erupted, shuddering through her body.

All thought shattered into a thousand tingling, prickling lights. Though she could hear herself crying out, her voice was far away, and she had no control over the wails escaping from her lips. The convulsions continued to surge, then as suddenly as they had started, they stopped.

She had a vague sense of him untying her ankles, then being lifted with the robe draped around her. When she opened her eyes she was curled up in his lap.

"Hey, darlin.'"

"Matt...that was unbelievable."

"I think you had multiple orgasms rolled into one."

"Where are we?"

"In Kevin's workroom. It was the closest place I could sit down and hold you."

"Wow," she said with a heavy sigh. "Talk about feeling weak. I'm not sure I can even walk."

"Take as long as you need to catch your breath, then we'll go up-stairs and get dressed. I know the perfect place to have dinner."

"What about Jinx?"

"I have some dog food here. He'll inhale it before we leave."

"Can I take a quick shower in that bathroom off the gym?"

"Sure, if you want."

"I do, but right now I just want to stay here," she murmured, sinking against him.

She never wanted to forget the moment. Closing her eyes and breathing in his scent, she knew the long-held crush she'd had on Matthew Montgomery had blossomed into love.

A LITTLE WHILE LATER, sitting in a booth across from each other in an intimate, family owned Italian restaurant, Matt and Dusty shared a generous helping of rich, cheesy lasagne and a bottle of red wine. It was the perfect meal to follow the passionate episode in the workroom.

The ambience was warm and cozy, the candle in the potbellied Chianti bottle flickered, and leaning back in the bench seat, Dusty let out a contented sigh.

"I think this is the most relaxed I've been in a very long time."

"Are you relaxed enough to meet my folks?" Matt asked, leaning across the table.

"That came out of nowhere," she said, abruptly sitting up. "I guess so."

"If you're not up for it, that's cool. I'll drop you at my house and swing back over there. I don't need much time."

"I'm definitely up for it, but why do I get the feeling there's more to this spontaneous visit to your parents than just wanting to stop in and say hello."

"Because there is. I don't trust this Slim Jim guy."

"Well, duh," she said, rolling her eyes. "What's there to trust?"

"I mean, something about this doesn't smell right."

"I don't understand."

"He caught me off guard today, and I don't believe that was an accident. He may come across like a lowlife drunk who doesn't know what he's doin', but I'm startin' to think that could be an act."

"How do you mean?"

"He came to the saddlery to give me his ultimatum. He must have known I'd be there alone at the end of the day, which means he's been watchin' my routine, and that surprises me. I'm suddenly not feelin' so confident about tomorrow. That's why I wanna talk to dad. He's the smartest man I ever met, and I need to get his take on things."

"Then of course I want to be there," Dusty exclaimed, "and I think you're right about that creep. At the show grounds he knew exactly what to say to freak me out, and what he yelled at you about me being a whiner or a screamer would make any man nuts. I'm amazed you didn't race out and punch him in the nose. Thank goodness you had the presence of mind to stay put."

"That's what I mean. I'm tellin' you, Dusty, there's more to him than meets the eye, and I don't wanna be caught with my pants down again."

"Then we should definitely talk to your dad on the way home. Will my car be safe in your parking lot?"

"As safe as anywhere. The lot is lit up like a football field, there are security cameras, and I have a patrol that drives by throughout the night. Speakin' of which, I'd better let them know your car is allowed to be there. Then I'll call my dad and make sure he's not too tired for us to stop in."

"Matt, you really are worried, aren't you?"

"Not worried exactly," he said thoughtfully. "Let's just say I don't wanna underestimate this guy, and I wanna stay a step ahead."

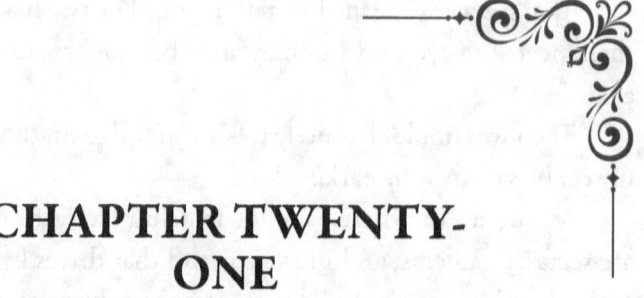

CHAPTER TWENTY-ONE

MATT'S PARENTS WERE thrilled with the prospect of meeting Dusty, but as Matt drove from town the mood in the truck was unusually quiet. Even Jinx napped in the seat behind them.

"Maybe I'm just being paranoid," Dusty muttered as they turned off the main road towards the lake, "but I think you might be right. I'm starting to feel that something is off too."

"Dad will figure it out. He has an uncanny way of seeing beyond the obvious."

"If he does I hope it's something we can deal with before tomorrow."

"Hey, take a deep breath. I know what happened in the parking lot was unexpected and upsetting, but—"

"You have a gift for understatement," Dusty muttered, cutting him off. "He was terrifying. I thought he was going to grab me and take me with him."

"That's exactly what he wanted you to think. Not that exactly, but he wanted to terrify you so you'd persuade me to part with twenty-five thousand dollars. It was just part of his game. I'm sure he's done the same thing to others in his checkered past. He also expected me to come charging out to save you. That part didn't work, but he still thinks he got what he wanted."

"Scaring me half to death and delivering his message?"

"That's right. You can't let him get under your skin. The way to beat guys like Jim Lewis is not to let them intimidate you."

"Kind of hard when he's leaning over you and spitting whiskey breath in your face," she said solemnly. "I should've kicked him in the nuts."

"I would've enjoyed seeing that," Matt said with a grin, as he turned into the driveway of his parents' large rambling house.

"If I ever find myself in that situation again, that's exactly what I'll do."

"Famous last words," Matt declared, coming to a stop. Jinx immediately sat up and barked. "He loves comin' here. Mom always has a marrow bone for him."

"Aren't you a lucky dog," Dusty said, reaching back and petting him.

The moment Matt climbed out, Jinx leapt into the front, jumped outside, and bounded ahead.

"Good grief, he does love it here," Dusty remarked.

As she stepped from the truck and walked up to Matt, the porch light turned on and the front door opened.

"Hello, sweetheart," his mother said happily, "and you must be Dusty," she continued as they approached.

"It's lovely to meet you, Mrs. Montgomery."

"Please, come in. Hello, Jinx. Yes, I have your bone," she said with a laugh as Jinx ran around her. "Matt, there's coffee and cookies in the den with your father."

"Thanks, mom, that sounds good. We just had dinner, but we didn't stay for dessert."

"I must congratulate you on your wonderful win, Dusty," his mother said enthusiastically. "You must be so excited."

"I am. It was such a thrill."

"Will you be going to the nationals?"

"I'm not sure. I'm certainly thinking about it. The trip though...it's so far."

"It's not at our show grounds, that's for sure. Matt, why don't you go ahead while I get Jinx his bone?"

"Sounds like a plan," he replied. "I'm suddenly, dyin' for that coffee."

Taking Dusty's hand, Matt led her down the hallway, and as they entered his father's sanctuary, he stood up to welcome them.

"A real pleasure," he said, kissing Dusty on each cheek. "I've heard a lot about you. Try one of those cookies. They were baked this afternoon. Oatmeal raisin. My wife's speciality."

"He says that about all her cookies," Matt said with a chuckle, "but that's only because it's hard to know which is the best."

"What a great problem to have!" Dusty remarked with a wide smile. "Mr. Montgomery, it's such an honor to meet the man who built Silver Streak Saddlery."

"Thank you, though the truth be told, it was just hard work. When Matt stepped in he took it to a whole other level. Now sit down and make yourself comfortable. Matt, you said this couldn't wait, so tell me what's on your mind?"

"It's about Black Lightnin' and this crook, Slim Jim," Matt began, sitting down and pouring the coffee. "I've figured out a way to deal with him, but he's sharper than I initially thought, and I have the feelin' I've missed something."

"I'm listenin.'"

"I believe Jim's wife let Dusty take Licorice because her husband was gonna be gone much longer than either of them had planned. When he threatened Dusty at the show grounds, and told her he was gonna take her horse, it occurred to me it was the first step in shakin' her down for money!"

"You're so clever," his mother remarked as she joined them. "Just like your father. Sorry, I didn't mean to interrupt. Keep going."

"Thanks, mom," he said with a grin. "Anyway, I figured he's been gone so long because he's either been in prison, or he's wanted by the FBI."

"Yep," his father said, nodding his head. "I was just thinkin' the same thing."

"It was amazing how fast I was able to reach an agent who knew all about Jim Lewis, and yeah, he's been on the run. When I told him I knew where Jim was livin', the agent said he'd rather lure Jim into a trap. I'm not sure why, and I didn't ask, but I'd already planned on offerin' Jim a bunch of money to leave Dusty alone, then set up a meetin' and have the cops there. I even made sure I knew the hauler Jim would use. When I told the agent, he was all for it."

"Sounds good so far. Keep talkin'."

"After everyone had left the saddlery tonight, Jim ambushed Dusty in the parkin' lot and demanded' twenty-five grand or he'd take the horse...and hurt her."

"That's dreadful," his mother said, shaking her head. "What an awful man."

"Yeah, he's pretty bad," Matt said, taking a sip of his coffee. "The meetin' is supposed to be at four o'clock at Patrick O'Neal's barn. He thinks the horse is boarded there. I haven't had a chance to call the agent yet, but that aside, I feel as if I'm missin' something. Am I, dad?"

Without speaking, Matt's father leaned back in his chair and closed his eyes. The room fell quiet, the only sounds the ticking of a grandfather clock in the hall, and Jinx gnawing on his bone. Slightly bewildered, Dusty glanced across at Matt. He smiled and winked back at her.

"Right! This is what I get," his father proclaimed, opening his eyes and sitting up. "You're dealin' with a snake, a slippery snake. Snakes are fast, and you never know which way they're gonna wriggle. This is what I think you missed, and this is what you should do."

As his father began to lay out his thoughts, Matt shook his head, feeling almost embarrassed.

"Dad, you never cease to amaze me. I had only half a plan."

"Hey, don't sell yourself short. It was sound, but you were thinkin' like a rational human bein'. This guy isn't rational, he's a snake. You've gotta think like him to beat him. Remember, a crook, whether in a shirt 'n tie or dirty old dungarees, won't be thinkin' like honest folk."

"Thank you so much, Mr. Montgomery," Dusty said earnestly. "Matt was right. He said you were the smartest man he ever met. Now I know why."

"Call me tomorrow and let me know how it all spills out."

"The minute it goes down," Matt promised, rising to his feet.

"When your father was building the company, there wasn't anyone who could outsmart him," his mother said proudly.

"There still isn't," Matt said with a chuckle.

"Except my wife," his father said, sending her a wink, then laughed out loud.

"You old devil," she retorted. "What am I going to do with you?"

"If you haven't figured that out after all these years, we've got ourselves a problem."

As he chortled at his own joke, Dusty impulsively jumped to her feet, and hurried across the room to kiss him on the cheek.

"Thank you again, Mr. Montgomery. You've saved our bacon."

"She's a keeper," he grinned, winking up at Matt.

"Don't embarrass them!" Matt's mother scolded. "Come along, you two, I'll walk you to the door before he comes out with anything else."

They left the room, Jinx following with his bone firmly between his jaws, and with goodbye hugs on the front porch, they headed to the truck.

"My gosh," Dusty exclaimed as they climbed in and Matt started the engine. "I love your parents. They're adorable, and your father is so smart."

"I told you. No-one can read people and situations like my dad. I knew he'd figure it out."

"But you were smart enough to know something wasn't right."

"I've got a long way to go before I reach his level, if I ever do."

"You will," she said firmly. "I know it."

IT WAS A SHORT DRIVE to Matt's home, and tired from their long day and eventful evening, they moved straight to the bedroom and climbed between the sheets. As Matt turned off the lamp on his night-stand, Dusty curled into his arms.

"You must be very happy your father's home," he murmured. "I know I am."

"It's wonderful, especially with the news he brought back with him."

"Do you think your mom and dad will want the house to them-selves again tomorrow night?" he asked hopefully.

"That's why your pleased he's back!" she exclaimed, shifting to look up at him.

"Partly," he said with a grin, "but can you blame me?"

"I said it before, and I'll say it again. You're incorrigible."

"Yep, but that's not an answer to my question. Will they want you out of the house again?"

"Not a chance. In fact, Dad will insist I stick around for a family night."

"Bummer."

"It's just as well," she said softly, snuggling closer. "I don't want you getting tired of me."

"As long as you've got those pink chaps in your bag, I won't be get-tin' tired of you."

Dusty giggled, then yawned.

"Speaking of tired, I'm suddenly exhausted."

"I bet you are. I'm feelin' pretty wiped out too. Nite,' darlin.'"

"Goodnight, Matt."

She was about to add, *I love you,* but caught herself just in tme.

AT THE RUNDOWN HOME on Cottontail Lane, Jim and Kathy Lewis were celebrating. They'd just finished their second bottle of sparkling wine, and Jim was cursing himself for not buying a third.

"Fuck. Have we got any beer left?"

"I can't remember," Kathy replied, "but I still don't think we should've cracked open the champagne. You know I'm superstitious about shit like that."

"You worry too much, woman. These people won't know what hit 'em."

"Are you sure Mexico is where we should go? What about, I dunno, Vermont or somewhere?"

"Trust me, you'll love it down there. I've got us a real nice place right near the beach, and after livin' there so long, I've made some friends—important friends. The best part though, the law won't be bothered comin' after me down there, just like they weren't bothered before, and with twenty-five grand, fuck, Kathy, we'll be livin' like fuckin' royalty."

"I'll be real happy to get outta this dump, that's for sure. Let the bank take this place. I don't give a shit."

"This time tomorrow we'll be on our way to good times."

"Shit, we're outta food," Kathy muttered, staring at the empty pizza boxes. "Should we order more?"

"Nah. Let's smoke some weed and crash."

Rising unsteadily to his feet, he staggered down the hall towards the bedroom.

"You sure you've got this figured out right?" Kathy asked, following him. "I don't want any more shit landin' on our heads."

"Hell, yeah. Now take your fuckin' clothes off. I wanna look at you naked while I get stoned."

CHAPTER TWENTY-TWO

"I LOVE WAKING UP IN your arms," Dusty purred, sinking to the divine feel of Matt holding her from behind and kneading her breasts. "I never want to get out of bed."

"Don't even try," Matt said huskily. "You stay right here until I give you permission to leave."

"What was it that famous old western star used to say? I can't remember her name. The sexy one with the sultry voice."

"Mae West?"

"That's the one, Mae West. Are you just happy to see me, or is that a banana in your pocket—or is it the other way around? The banana bit first."

"Um, not sure, and it doesn't matter 'cos there are no pockets in this bed, or bananas," he said with a chuckle, then shifting her body, laid on top of her.

"Then that must be a six-shooter pressing against me."

"Yep, and it's comin' to visit," he growled, reaching across to the nightstand for a condom.

"I'm going on the pill."

"I wish you would," he declared, kneeling up and slipping the thin sheath over his rigid cock. "Where were we?"

"You said something about your six-shooter paying me a visit."

"Ah, so I did, and here it comes."

As his stiff member thrust inside her, Dusty closed her eyes and lifted her arms above her head. Just as she hoped, his fingers wrapped around her wrists, pinning them down.

"Ooh, Matt, I love it when you do that."

"One of these nights I'm gonna tie you to this bed, arms and legs wide apart, and tease you for a really...long...time," he breathed, stroking forcefully. "I might even introduce you to some of my wicked toys."

"What toys?" she asked breathlessly. "Please tell me."

"You met one of them last night when you were over the saddle. It made you crazy, didn't it Dusty?"

"Yes," she panted, "yes, it made me crazy, and so is talking to me like this."

"You'll be blindfolded and helpless," he continued, quickening the speed and force of his thrusts. "Totally, utterly helpless."

"Matt, you're making me—"

"I've got more to show you, a lot more," he muttered, interrupting "and your lovely tits are gonna meet toys made just for them."

"I'm s-so...c-close."

"Very soon you're gonna be close over and over again...'til you're beggin."

The glorious tingles suddenly pulsed through her body, and with his fingers clenching her wrists, she heard him groan through his climax.

"Good Lord, woman," he panted, his member slipping from her depths as the sparking sensations finally waned. "I'm not sure I'll survive this." Rolling off her body onto his back, he let out a heavy sigh. "My heart is poundin."

She laid still for a moment, catching her breath.

"You okay, darlin.'"

"I'm floating," she managed. "It's heavenly."

"Come closer."

"I can't move."

"Try."

Managing to shift her body, she curled against him and threw her arm over his chest.

"You're right," she mumbled. "This is much better."

But Jinx decided it was time for them to rise and shine. Putting his paws on the side of the bed, he leaned his head forward and voraciously licked Matt's arm, then barked.

"No, no, Jinx," Matt muttered. "Go away."

Refusing to be put off, Jinx barked again.

"Jinxy, can't you wait just a minute?" Dusty begged. "Please!"

He answered by climbing on the bed and crawling over Matt to reach her.

"Dammit, Jinx," Matt shouted, "get off."

Completely ignoring the command, Jinx stood over Dusty and began kissing her face. Laughing hysterically, she tried to push him away, but he wouldn't budge.

"Jinx. Off the bed!" Matt repeated. "Now."

Letting out a whine, his dog stopped, looked at him, then sent his tongue across Matt's nose.

"No, no!" Matt protested, but in his attempt to shove him off, he pushed him back on Dusty.

The rambunctious dog decided this was a wonderful game, and began jumping between them, barking and vigorously wagging his very large tail.

"And here I thought you had a well-trained dog," Dusty exclaimed, spitting out the words between peals of laughter.

"I never said I had a well-trained dog," Matt retorted, managing to climb from the bed. "Come on, Jinx, outside."

Excitedly leaping from the bed, he raced past Matt and led him down the hallway into the kitchen.

"What's gotten into you this morning?" Matt muttered, opening the back door.

Turning on the coffee-maker, he walked back to the bedroom quietly chuckling, but he found Dusty gone from the bed, and heard the shower running. He was about to amble into the bathroom to join her, when a profound realization swept over him.

"I'm happy. I'm really happy," he mumbled, then pausing, he added, Damn. I'm crazy in love with her."

The shower turned off, and a moment later Dusty appeared with a towel wrapped around her chest, and her wet hair falling around her shoulders. He thought she'd never looked more beautiful.

"What?" she asked. "Why are you looking at me like that."

"No reason," he replied quickly, bringing her into his arms and hugging her tightly.

THE EPIPHANY CONTINUED to haunt Matt through breakfast. He found himself glancing across at her, and as they cleaned up the dishes, he impulsively kissed her, then gazed at her as the deep feelings washed over him.

"Matt, are you sure you're okay? Is there something going on you're not telling me?"

"I'm just glad you're here."

Tilting her head, she studied him.

"Are you worried about today?"

"No, why?"

"You're being a bit weird."

"I am?"

"You know you are," she said, letting out a sigh. "Please tell me what it is."

"Okay, there is something," he admitted, not wanting to lie to her, but not yet ready to share what was in his heart. "It's has nothin' to with what's goin' down today, and it's not a bad thing, not at all. I promise I'll tell you later. I just need to think on it a bit more."

"Thank you. Later is fine, but I won't let you off the hook."

"I'm sure you won't," he said with a smile, thinking her choice of words was interesting. "I hate to say this, but it's about time we took off."

"I know. I just need to get my bag."

"I'll meet you at the truck. Come on, Jinx. Let's hit the road."

Matt entered the garage and rolled up the door, then settling behind the wheel, he watched her as she came out of the house. She took his breath away.

"I've gotta get this right, Jinx," he mumbled under his breath. "I can't let anything happen to her or her horse."

"Do you want to drop me at the show, or take me to my car?" she asked as she climbed in.

"I've been thinkin' on that," he replied, backing on to the street. "If Jim Lewis swings by Silver Streak and sees your car in the lot, he'll assume you're not at the show.

"Oh, good point."

"Will you be able to meet up for lunch?"

"For sure. Our last class is at ten o'clock, then we'll be finished. The horses and their tack will be loaded up and taken back to the barn. Patrick will put the last bits and pieces in his car. There's hardly anything left."

"Can you ask him to drop you off at Annie's? If you call me when you're leaving, I'll meet you there, then I'll take you back to your car. But I'll want to follow you home."

"Do you think that's really necessary?"

"I'm not takin' any chances," he replied, shooting her a look. "Dad was right. Lewis is a snake. I wouldn't put anything past him."

"When this is over, I'm buying him a very special gift. I don't know what that could be, but I'll find him something."

AS DUSTY AND MATT ARRIVED at the show grounds, Slim Jim was stumbling out of bed. Kathy, a canteen worker, had just called her supervisor to hand in her notice and make arrangements to pick up her last check.

"We've only got one suitcase and your backpack," she declared, walking in and staring at the clothes scattered around the room.

"Just take whatever," Jim muttered, running his hands over his face. "We'll buy new stuff after we cross the border. Shit is so much cheaper down there. I'm gonna rinse off."

"Do you want any of the crap on the shelves? The pictures and stuff?"

"Nah. Just leave it," he grunted, staggering past her. "Make me some fresh coffee, then I'm goin' into town and gassin' up the car."

"Can you take me by work to pick up my wages? It will be much easier than taking the bus."

"Yeah, but call and make sure you don't have to wait, and no hangin' around for long goodbyes."

Pulling off his boxers and stumbling into the shower, an evil smile twisted his lips.

"Won't be long now. A few hours and I'll be sittin' pretty. Fuckin' morons. This is almost too easy."

Had he not been so hungover, or narcissistic, or greedy, he might have listened to the wisdom of his words.

IT WAS JUST PAST NOON when Matt heard from Dusty. The morning had been busy and successful, and she was on her way to Annie's with Patrick. Hurrying from his office, Jinx excitedly trotting along beside him, he made his way through the workroom and into reception.

"Just off for lunch," he said, waving to Jeanette as he passed. "Call me if you need me."

Moving outside, Matt paused to scan his surroundings. Seeing nothing of note, he climbed into his truck and left the parking lot, his eyes scrutinizing the street. Reaching the cafe, he saw Patrick's car drive off as he parked. Moving quickly around to the patio entrance, he spotted her at a table under the sprawling oak.

"Hey, beautiful," he said, kissing her on the cheek before sitting down. "You said on the phone you had a successful morning. Does that mean another blue ribbon?"

"Of course. The girls did really well," she replied. "It was hard for me to stay focused though, with everything that's going on."

"I'm sure. How are you holdin' up?"

"Good, considering. I just wish that creep was in custody and we could get on with our lives."

"I know, darlin', and it's gonna be okay. All of it will, and I do mean, all of it."

"I'm so glad dad's home," she said with a sigh. "I feel so much better knowing he's at the house with Licorice. Matt, what would I have done if you hadn't come along? It's like a miracle. No! I take that back. It is a miracle. You're saving Licorice and me."

As he sensed the depth of her feelings, he wanted to share his, but it wasn't the right time.

"I agree, it is a miracle, and just as much for me as it is for you," he said softly, leaning across the table.

As she smiled at him, his heart swelled, but Mary Jo arrived to take their order, and the moment was broken.

"Could you put a rush on that?" he asked as she picked up their menus.

"Sure thing."

"Are you in a hurry?" Dusty asked.

"We both are," he replied. "I need to get you home safely so you can bring your dad up to date, and the next couple of hours will fly by."

"I guess you're right."

"I have to get back to my office and make sure there aren't any last minute hiccups."

"Matt, are you on edge?"

"No, not on edge. I'm fired up. I can't wait to see this dirtbag get what's comin' to him."

"You and me both," she muttered, "and I really wish I'd kicked him in the nuts!"

CONSTANTLY CHECKING his rear view mirror, Matt followed Dusty back to her house then returned to Silver Streak. Not seeing any battered old cars parked on the street or in the parking lot, he pulled into his space and strode into the building.

Anxious, but confident, he hurried to his office. As Jinx curled into his bed, Matt retrieved his cell phone from his pocket and settled behind his desk, quickly placing a call to Rod at Circus Farms.

"Just checkin' in," Matt declared as Rod picked up. "Is everything still on track?"

"Yep, in fact Jim called to confirm he'd be here at three-thirty. Funny thing, though, when he came in to book the rig he didn't give me any details, but on the phone he said there might be trouble 'cos the horse we had to pick up had been stolen from him. He even said he has the paperwork to prove it."

"No kiddin'. He must have forged something. What did you say?"

"That it was none of my business, and once the horse was loaded I'd drive him wherever he wanted."

"I really appreciate this, Rod."

"Like I said when you first told me about what happened, I can't stand dirtbags who pull crap like this, especially ones who threaten women."

"Yeah, this guy is a real snake. Don't take your eyes off him."

"I'm gonna have Trevor follow us."

"Good idea, but I doubt you'll need him. The agents will be around if there are any problems."

"Matt, this is a piece of cake. You've got everything set up so well this guy doesn't have a hope in hell."

"I believe that, but I can't get my heart to stop jumpin.'"

"You're just concerned about the girl caught in the middle. I'll tell you what you probably told her. Don't worry, this will be over real quick."

"You're right. That's exactly what I said! Rod, you're a pal. Thanks."

"Hey—glad to help catch this scumbag. I'll see you in the trenches."

The call ended, and Matt let out a heavy breath.

"I need to workout," he muttered. "Come on, Jinx. I'm gonna hit the gym for an hour."

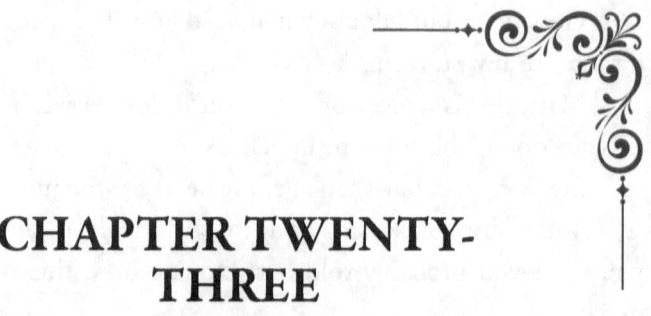

CHAPTER TWENTY-THREE

IT WAS 3:30 P.M. LEANING against his truck ready to leave, Rod felt his pulse tick up as the battered Chevy rolled into the parking area. "Hey," Jim Lewis called, stepping from his car and walking up to him.

"Hey, there," Rod replied, looking for any bulges that suggested a concealed weapon, but the man was thin, and his shirt hung loose around his body. "You wanna ride with me or follow?" Rod continued, climbing into his truck.

"I'll ride with you," Jim said, jumping in next to him.

Buckling up and starting the powerful engine, Rod rolled into the main road. Glancing in his side mirror he suppressed a smile. Pulling from a parking space in his black sedan, Trevor, his powerfully built, right hand man fell in behind him.

WHILE THE RIG CRUISED down Main Street, Matt turned down the gravel driveway into Patrick's barn. Nearing the entrance to the stable yard, Patrick appeared from inside and waved Matt to a parking space next to the riding ring. Leaving Jinx in the truck, Matt climbed out and looked back towards the gate. Two dark blue SUV's with heavily tinted windows were heading towards them.

"Right on time," he remarked, looking over at Patrick. "Let the games begin."

"As you say," Patrick murmured, "and to the winner goes the spoils."

SLOWING AT A RED LIGHT near the edge of town, Rod looked across at the unkempt man beside him. He smelled of cigarettes and whiskey. "Glad the traffic's not heavy," Rod remarked. "We may be a small town, but it can get busy."

"Uh-huh," Jim grunted. "Turn left at the next corner."

"Left?"

"Yep."

"I thought we were going to Patrick O'Neal's Stables."

"There's been a change of plan. The horse was moved."

"Whatever you say," Rod replied, hoping his voice sounded casual.

The light turned green. Driving forward and into the left hand turn lane at the next street, he noticed Jim was studying his side mirror. Rod gently pumped his brakes three times, the signal that Jim might suspect they were being followed. As the black sedan traveled past them and continued straight ahead, Rod saw his passenger noticeably relax.

THE DARK BLUE SUV'S were parked behind the barn out of sight. Perched on the fence of the riding ring, Matt and Patrick watched a faded red, compact car turn into the driveway. Traveling slowly forward, it stopped in front of them, and a disheveled, overweight woman with badly bleached blonde hair stepped out.

"Excuse me," Patrick said, walking up to her. "Haven't we met before?"

"Yeah. I'm Kathy Lewis. You came to my house with that girl and screwed me and my husband on that horse. Now I'm here to collect the money."

"I don't understand," Matt exclaimed, stepping forward. "He was supposed to be here, and where's the trailer?"

"Hand over the money and I'll tell ya," she replied, narrowing her eyes and staring up at him.

"This isn't what we arranged."

"Hey, I'm callin' the shots," she barked, "and you don't wanna piss me off! I know that fuckin' horse isn't here, and if you wanna see it again you'd better hand over the cash."

"Matt, we should just do what she says," Patrick said solemnly.

"This is bullshit!" Matt shouted. "Don't screw with me, or I'll—"

"You'll do what?" she snapped. "Nothin'. That's what. You think we're stupid? We know exactly where that horse is, and if you want that girl to keep it, you're gonna hand over that fuckin' money. Every damn penny. Now quit stallin'."

"Come on, Matt," Patrick said, his voice grim. "We've got no choice."

"How can we trust her after they've pulled this stunt? I could hand over the cash and Jim could still take the horse."

"Hey, if anyone's pullin' bullshit around here, it's you!" the woman screeched. "The horse isn't here, but it don't matter, 'cos Jim *is* over at your girlfriend's house with a trailer ready to haul it away. Now hand over the cash!"

"Come on, Matt," Patrick said urgently. "We have no choice."

"Dammit," Matt muttered, glowering at the woman. "Okay, but I'm warnin' you, if your husband hurts Dusty or touches a hair on that horse, I'll hunt you both down and it won't end well. You hear me?"

"Then you'd better hand over the money so that don't happen!"

"Let's just get this done," Patrick interjected, stepping between them.

Throwing up his hands, Matt turned sharply and marched into the barn with Patrick and Kathy following. Entering Patrick's office, he pulled a leather bag from a cupboard, placed it on Patrick's desk and unzipped it.

"There!" he exclaimed. "Twenty-five thousand dollars in cash."

Moving forward, Kathy Lewis peered inside, lifted out a wad of notes, fanned it with her thumb, then tossed it back inside.

"Did you really think you could pull a fast one on us?" she cackled. "What a couple of morons you are. Now I'm leavin', and if I don't call Jim and tell him I'm safely on my way and no-one is followin' me, you're gonna have a real misery party. You get my drift?"

"Just so I understand this," Matt said slowly, "your husband is over at Dusty Anderson's home right now, and if I don't give you this cash, you steal her horse."

"Isn't that what I've been telling you? What are you, a dumbass?"

Grabbing the bag and taking quick, short steps, she hurried from the office and into the barn aisle.

A hand grabbed her arm.

"Kathleen Lewis, you're under arrest."

Bolting out the door, Matt sprinted to his truck, jumped in, and peeled off down the driveway.

DRIVING THE RIG SLOWLY through the residential neighborhood, Rod was doing his best to stay calm, but it wasn't easy. Jim was fidgeting in his seat, and he'd unbuckled his seatbelt.

"I like this neighborhood," Rod remarked, pretending to look at the modest homes. "There are some great little ranches back here with some decent acreage, and there are trails up those hills."

"Three more blocks, turn right." Jim said brusquely.

"Where will we be taking this horse once we pick it up?"

"I'll tell you once we start movin'."

"I only ask because I need to let my office know when to expect me back," Rod continued, turning into Dusty's street.

"See that big oak tree on the corner. Just past it you'll see a wide area where you can park. I'll go get the horse and walk him out. You open up the back of the trailer."

"Sure thing."

Reaching the tree, Rod pulled into the open area and cut the engine.

"Don't you need a halter?"

Without responding, Jim climbed out of the truck.

JIM LEWIS HAD STUDIED the comings and goings of Karen Anderson and her daughter. He knew there were cans loaded up behind the gate, but they'd be easily dealt with. He also knew Karen Anderson was gone all day, and if Dusty was home he'd have a little fun with her before taking the horse and hitting the road.

Another trailer waited ten miles down the interstate just off the freeway. His dutiful wife would meet him there with the cash she'd picked up at Patrick O'Neal's barn, and there was another fifteen grand waiting when he dropped off the horse a couple of hours away. He'd have forty-grand in his pocket.

Easily jumping the fence, he went directly to the cans and lifted the one at the top. To his shock, the entire pile collapsed in a clanging, clattering mess. His heart leaping, he jumped back and darted his eyes to the house.

The curtains were drawn.

The house appeared to be empty.

"Stupid bitch," he grunted. "What good is your stupid fuckin' burglar alarm if there's no-one here!"

Quickly dragging the cans out of the way, he pulled a small, metal rod from his back pocket, unlocked the padlock, then marched to the paddock where Licorice was grazing. Spying a small shed, he pushed open the door and grinned. He hadn't known it was the tack room, but he'd figured there'd be one close by. Grabbing a halter and stuffing some carrots into his pockets, he headed out to the paddock.

"MATT, THANK GOD! WHERE are you?" Dusty asked urgently, answering her phone as she peered through the curtains from the kitchen.

"Real close. What's goin' on?"

"Jim Lewis is here. He's in the paddock with Licorice."

"I'm turnin' in your driveway."

"Okay."

Ending the call as she ran through the house, she unlocked the front door to see Matt jogging towards her with Jinx running along beside him.

"Thank goodness you made it in time," Dusty exclaimed as he hurried inside.

"I knew it was gonna be close."

"Quick, come and watch with mom and dad."

Moving swiftly through the house, Dusty led him into the master bedroom where her parents peeked through a crack in the drapes.

"HEY, LIGHTNIN', REMEMBER me?" Jim said softly, holding out a carrot as he approached the big, black gelding.

Lifting his head, Licorice pricked his ears, snorted, then smelling the treat, he ambled forward and gobbled it up.

"Carrots make horse thievin' so fuckin' easy," Jim chuckled as he slipped the halter over the horse's head. "Come on, there's plenty more where that came from."

Licorice took a step, then jerked his head up and refused to move.

"What the fuck are you doin'?" Jim yelled, tugging on the lead rope. "Dammit. Here's another carrot."

Though tossing his head, Licorice stopped long enough to gobble it down.

"Are we good now?" Jim asked, feeding him another. "Come on. Let's take a walk."

Jim started into the backyard, and though letting out a loud snort, the horse followed, but as they approached the gate, Licorice planted his feet.

Jim took a breath.

Losing his temper wouldn't help.

He fished in his pocket for the last treat.

Turning to face the stubborn horse, Jim held it out in front of him, and walked slowly backwards.

"Come on, big fella," he coaxed, leading him through the gate with the carrot. "Just a few more steps."

They were through.

"Hello, Jim!"

He spun around.

A man wearing an FBI vest had his gun pointing at him.

Frantically looking around, he spied unmarked cars blocking the street on either side.

"It's over, Lewis," the agent declared. "Drop the lead rope, slowly put your hands behind your head, get on your knees, then sprawl on the ground."

But Licorice wanted no part of the drama.

With a loud whinny, he suddenly reared, and jerking the lead rope free, he bolted into the street.

The distraction was all Jim needed.

Darting back through the gate, he took off running.

WHILE JIM HAD BEEN trying to get Licorice through the gate, Matt, Dusty and her parents had hurried back into the kitchen, Jinx following along behind. Assuming Jim had been arrested, they pulled back the drapes and opened the sliding glass door, only to see Jim sprinting through the yard.

"Where's Licorice," Dusty immediately wailed, dashing outside before anyone could stop her.

"Dusty, come back" Matt yelled, but terrified something had happened to her precious horse there was no stopping her.

"Where are the agents?" Tom exclaimed, watching Jim race towards the paddock. "He's getting away."

"He's not goin' anywhere," Matt growled, grabbing Jinx by the collar and pointing to the fleeing criminal. "Get him, Jinx, go get him."

Leaping from the patio, Jinx took off after his prey.

"Go after your dog," Tom said quickly. "I'll take care of my daughter."

AS SEVERAL AGENTS RAN past her and into the backyard, Dusty looked frantically up and down the street for Licorice. Finally spotting him in the shadow of a tree, she realized he was tied to a rig, calmly eating from a hay net, and flanked on either side by two cowboys. Overwhelmed with relief, she hurried down the block.

"Is he okay," she asked breathlessly as she drew near.

"Sure, he's fine, and you must be Dusty. I'm Rod Clark."

"Thank you so much," she panted, hugging her horse's neck. "Are you all right, big boy?"

"He is, but you're not," Rod replied with a grin. "Catch your breath a minute. Those agents will catch that jerk, no problem. They have this whole area cordoned off. The only place your horse is goin' is back to his paddock."

JIM'S LONG LEGS HAD carried him swiftly through the paddock to the first gate. Stopping to open it, he glanced quickly over his shoulder. To his horror he saw Matt's black and white dog galloping towards him.

But that wasn't all.

Running at a fast clip Matt wasn't far behind, and several agents were already entering the paddock.

Turning back to the gate, he cursed under his breath. The latch refused to flip up. He'd have to climb over. As he grabbed the iron bar across the top and hoisted himself up, he heard a snarl.

He kicked out.

The threatening foot missed Jinx's head by inches.

Jinx attacked, sinking his teeth into Jim's calf.

Letting out a shriek, Jim's fingers slipped from the gate and he fell to the ground.

"Get off me, get off me," he howled, his arms flailing.

"Back, Jinx, back," Matt called, almost upon them.

"Fuck! Fuck! Get him off."

Slowing to a walk, Matt took his time as he moved forward and grabbed his dog's collar.

"Jinx, lie down," he ordered, pulling him back. "Stay."

The dog immediately dropped on his stomach.

Looking across to the paddock, Matt could see the agents were still a distance away. Taking a breath, he leaned down, grabbed Jim by the shirt, and punched him squarely in the nose.

"That's from Dusty," he growled, then punching him a second time in the gut, he added, "and that's from me."

CHAPTER TWENTY-FOUR

THE AGENTS ARRIVED, and Jim Lewis was handcuffed, pulled to his feet, and read his rights. Matt was about to head back to the house when he was approached by a tall man with a crew cut. Matt thought he resembled a marine sergeant out of an old World War II movie.

"Agent Stafford," the man announced. "We prefer civilians stay out of the way, but in this case I'm glad you stepped in."

"Matt Montgomery," Matt replied. "It's good to meet you."

"I figured that's who you were. Mr. Montgomery, your dog's a hero. With all this brush around here Lewis might have given us the slip. It wouldn't be the first time," he said with a deep frown, then breaking into a grin and lowering his voice, he added, "Too bad he hit his face on that gate when he fell off."

"Yeah, too bad," Matt murmured, grinning back. "As far as my dog goes, he can be a rascal, but he's the best. Oh, would you excuse me? There's Dusty with her horse," Matt declared, suddenly spying her walking into the backyard with Licorice. "Can we finish this later?"

"Sure," the agent said with a nod. "I just wanted to say thanks. Someone will be in touch about getting your statement."

Matt started back, Jinx trotting along by his side, but the moment Jinx saw Dusty he bounded ahead. Breaking into a jog Matt followed, but, a balding, older agent intercepted him.

"Excuse me. Matt Montgomery? I'm Special Agent Gary Fisher."

"Agent Fisher, it's good to meet you in person," Matt declared, stopping and shaking his hand. "I was gonna search you out. Thanks for makin' all this happen."

"I'm the one who should be thanking you. Like I told you on the phone, we've been after this guy for years. When you called we couldn't believe our luck."

"If you're gonna be in town a while I'd love to meet up," Matt said hastily. "I don't mean to be rude, but I have to see Dusty."

"No problem, By the way, John Draper is here. He was in one of the cars. The three of us should get together."

"That sounds like a plan. Just call me and let me know. I'll be there."

"Will do. Now go see that girl of yours."

Running into the backyard, Matt saw her standing in front of the patio as her parents spoke with an agent. Turning her head, she broke into a smile and waved, then leading Licorice, she hurried across to meet him.

"I'm so glad this is all over," she exclaimed as he hugged her.

"Are you all right, darlin'?"

"Yes, fine, and so is Licorice, thank goodness. I need to get him back to his paddock though. Will you come with me?"

"You bet. Where was he when you found him?"

"Rod had him at his trailer with—."

"Me!"

An attractive man with a thick head of salt and pepper hair had marched up.

"Hi. I'm John Draper."

"John!" Matt exclaimed. "I'm so glad you could get out here for this."

"After everything Jim Lewis put me through I wouldn't have missed it," he said gravely as the trio began walking. "I can't tell you how grateful I am you tracked me down. Seeing Lightning again—it's unreal. I was never much of a rider, but I loved all my horses, especially this guy," he murmured, placing his hand on the horse's neck as they continued forward. "He was very special to me, and knowing how well he's been taken care of, I can't tell you how relieved I am."

"I don't know how long he was with that creep, but Licorice couldn't get in the trailer fast enough when we picked him up," Dusty remarked, "and he sure didn't look like he does now."

"He's very lucky you found him. I'll always be thankful you came to his rescue."

"I can't believe Jim Lewis tried to get away," Dusty muttered, shaking her head. "I wish I could've been the one to stop him."

"Dusty," John began solemnly, "you bought my horse from the people who stole him, and I'm not sure what that means in terms of legal ownership. We must get together before I leave town. Give me a dollar, and I'll give you a bill of sale, then you can be sure this big, beautiful boy will be one-hundred percent yours."

"Oh, my gosh, thank you so much. Licorice means the world to me."

"That's obvious, and you deserve the peace of mind. I'll certainly be sleeping better at night. Lightning—sorry—Licorice—has found himself a wonderful home."

"You can visit him any time you want. Why don't you come to the nationals and watch us? Though I'm still not a hundred percent sure I'll be going."

"Let me know. Maybe I will. I'd love to see him in action again."

They had reached the paddock, and Dusty spotted the agents helping Jim Lewis walk across the paddock.

"Good grief! What happened to him?" Dusty asked, shocked by the man's appearance. "Is that blood on his face? I wonder why he's limping?"

"Jinx did that," Matt said with a grin. "He's the hero of the day."

"He is? Tell me everything?"

"When Jim took off, it was Jinx who caught up with him."

"Ouch," she said with a laugh. "I love it!"

"Ouch is right!" Matt exclaimed. "Jim was climbing over the gate and tried to kick Jinx—and—well—Jinx wasn't too happy about that. He went after Jim's leg and got him real good. When Jim fell off the gate he must have hit his nose on the solid metal bar at the top."

"Is that right?" John said, raising his eyebrows. "Excellent."

"I thought so," Matt agreed. "I'm not sure why, but when his nose hit the gate, my knuckles twinged."

Dusty gasped, staring at him with wide eyes.

"Matt! You didn't!"

"I told him the punch in the nose was for you, then I gave him one in the gut from me."

"You're a lucky guy, Matt," John said with a grimace. "I was stuck in the back of an SUV and they wouldn't let me out!"

"You and Jinx. My two heroes," Dusty exclaimed, leaning down to make a fuss of the happy border collie, but straightening up she noticed John was staring at the agents. "John, is something wrong?"

"Everything is finally right," he replied, "but I need to have a word with that scumbag."

As Dusty removed the halter and let Licorice wander away, Itsy and Bitsy appeared from behind some bushes. Bleating up a storm, they trotted over to join him.

"Poor things must have been so scared with all the ruckus," Dusty said with a sigh.

"I'm sure you're right, but it looks like a happy reunion."

"That won't be," she remarked, nodding towards John as he approached Jim Lewis. "I want to hear this."

Moving quickly after him, they stood close enough to listen.

"It's been over four years since you stole my horse, ruined my reputation, and screwed up my business," John growled. "It took me a long time to clean up the mess you left behind, but I knew this day would come, and somehow I knew it would be Lightning that would make it happen. I'm going to do everything in my power to make sure you go down for a long time, and one more thing! May you rot in the fires of hell."

Dusty expected a nasty retort, but the man who had terrified her and turned her life upside down, remained silent with his eyes on the ground.

"Come on, Lewis," one of the agents said. "Move!"

"I need to go with them," John said, turning back to Dusty and Matt, "but I'll be in touch soon."

As John followed the agents, Matt pulled Dusty into his arms and hugged her tightly.

"It's over," he murmured. "Now you can enjoy your father's home-coming, and you can also make up your mind about the nationals."

"I'm still not sure about that, but I have made a decision about be-coming a professional. Thank you so much for offering to sponsor me, but—"

"You don't wanna be on the road," Matt interjected.

"No. It's not for me. Besides, I'd miss you too much."

"Back at ya, darlin'. I'd still like to feature you in our advertisin'."

"Really?"

"Absolutely. I told you earlier, you've got a brand. You're the girl in the pink chaps. I was even thinkin' Silver Streak could design a saddle incorporatin' that, but right now, why don't we go back to the house and have a cup of coffee with your folks. I sure could use one."

"Yes, please. I can't wait to sit down."

"Uh, Dusty, before we go—I know you're gonna be with your mom and dad tonight, and I can't wait another minute to tell you this. The thing is..."

"Are you going to tell me what you were thinking about this morn-ing—why you were so preoccupied?"

"I guess I am," he mumbled, shuffling his feet.

"You said it's not bad, but you're frowning."

"Dammit, I'm not doin' this real well."

"This isn't like you. Just tell me, Matt."

"So, uh, the thing is," he said softly, taking her hands, "this is the first time I've ever said this. I want you to know that."

"You're kind of freaking me out. Can you please just tell me?"

"Dot, Dusty, whatever you wanna call yourself, I'm in love with you, In fact, I love you like crazy."

THE AGENTS HAD CLEARED the backyard, and Karen and Tom had just said goodbye to Special Agent Gary Fisher when they heard Dusty squeal. Panicked, they looked across to the paddock. Matt had lifted Dusty off the ground and was holding her in a bear hug.

"I think our daughter just got some more good news," Karen remarked with a grin.

"Looks like it," he said wistfully. "Seems like yesterday she was a skinny kid with braces and glasses, then I came back from a haul and my Dot had become Dusty, a beautiful young woman. Now it looks like she's found herself a man."

"Not just any man, he's the one," Karen murmured. "If he makes her as happy as you've made me," she continued, staring up at her husband, "she'll be one very lucky girl."

CHAPTER TWENTY-FIVE

Two Weeks Later

STANDING IN MATT'S bedroom, Dusty gazed out at the still lake and slumped her shoulders.

"I think it's about time you told me what's goin' on with you," Matt murmured, walking up and hugging her from behind.

"I didn't hear you come in," she said softly. "I love it up here. It's so peaceful."

"That's not an answer."

She paused.

"Uh, just stuff."

"You haven't been my happy girl for several days. You need to tell me what's wrong."

"It's nothing," she said, feigning a smile and facing him.

"This ends now," he said firmly, taking her hand and leading her to the bed. "Drop the jeans."

"What? Why?"

"You heard me," he replied, sitting on the edge of the mattress, "or would you prefer I order you to put on your chaps?"

She let out a resigned sigh. Wearing the chaps meant the hairbrush. Quickly kicking off her shoes and unzipping her jeans, she pushed them down her legs and tossed them aside.

"Over my knee."

"This isn't necessary," she muttered, crawling across his lap, but as she settled into position, she knew it was what she'd been waiting for.

"I'm gonna warm your backside, then you're gonna tell me what's been botherin' you."

"You don't have to, I'll just tell—ow."

"Good, I'm glad you're already seein' sense," he declared, interrupting her with a slap, "but you're still gonna get a spankin'. We both know you need it."

Raising his hand, he delivered a quick volley of stinging smacks, then paused to rub her hot skin.

"You were right," she mumbled, softly moaning as she sank into his lap.

"About what?"

"Doing this."

"All you've gotta do is ask," he said softly, sliding her white lace panties down her legs. "A little more on your bare backside."

Though she squirmed and yelped, he landed a dozen slow, hard slaps.

"We're done," he murmured, beginning his comforting caress. "Catch your breath and relax."

Closing her eyes, she let out a long, low moan and sank into his lap. The tension had left her body, and she knew she'd be able to tell him.

"Matt, I—"

"Come and lie next to me," he said softly, helping her on to the bed and pulling her into his arms. "Okay, darlin'. What's the problem?"

"It's about the nationals," she whispered. "I don't want to go."

"Ah, I see."

"Everyone is expecting me to, especially now they know Licorice was such a big deal when he was back east. If I don't go, Dad would be so disappointed, and Patrick—oh my gosh—he'd be really upset, but the worst thing is, I'd be letting you down."

"Whoa, what are you talkin' about? Why would you be lettin' me down?"

"Silver Streak. I'd be letting Silver Streak down," she exclaimed, then burying her head in his chest she dissolved into tears. "I'm totally screwed. There's no answer."

"Tell me why you don't wanna go."

"I don't want Licorice to travel halfway across the country just so I can compete. He could get stuck in some freak early snow storm—or worse! Why put him at risk and go to all that trouble and expense when I don't really care about it, but I feel like I have no choice?"

"Of course you do, and if you really don't want to go, your heart won't be in it and you won't do well."

"No, I won't, but—"

"There is no but, and I'm sorry you've been feelin' so much pressure."

"Pressure. That's exactly what it is. My stomach's been upset, I haven't been able to sleep, and—"

"Stop! It's over, and believe me, not only will everyone understand, they'll feel terrible you've been torturin' yourself like this. They were excited because they thought you were."

"You think so?"

"Absolutely, and there's always next year."

"But what about advertising for Silver Streak?"

"Don't give that a second's thought."

Wiping her face, she shifted her body to look at him.

"Next year—that sounds good. Maybe I'm feeling like this because of all the crap that happened. All I know is, competing at the nationals is the last thing I want to do right now."

"Then you won't. If this isn't the time, it isn't, and it's no big deal."

"Matt, I love you so much," she sniffled, wrapping her arms around his neck. "Thank you. You always know the right thing to say."

"Do you have anything else on your mind? Is that everything?"

"Uh...not exactly."

"I had a feelin' there might be more. We're not leavin' this bed until I hear it all."

"I'm not sure how to say this."

"Do you need to go back over my knee?"

"No! Okay here goes. I'm totally excited you want me to move in with you."

"But...?"

"But I can't stand the thought of not being able to step outside and give Licorice a carrot, or take him on the trail. I don't want him boarded anywhere, not even with Patrick. I'm sorry, Matt, this is so hard. I want to be with both of you. I need to be with both of you."

"Was that so difficult?"

"Yes, it was! And it is!"

"I told you a while back I'd love to have my horse in my backyard. I meant it, and you and Licorice belong together. I have the answer for both of us. I was gonna surprise you over dinner tonight."

"I can't imagine...tell me!"

"I was gonna mention this sooner, but I wanted everything settled before I did, and this mornin' I got the nod. At first I was thinkin' I'd buy the Lewis's place, but it needs so much work, and the thought of livin' there with all that bad energy, sound's kinda crazy but—"

"I totally agree," Dusty said earnestly. "It's a great piece of property but it would be too weird."

"Exactly, so, I'm swappin' houses with mom and dad. They've been wantin' to downsize for a while, and this place is perfect for them."

"But they don't have a barn, do they?"

"Not yet, but they do have just over five acres. That's what I needed to check out. The zoning for having horses and outbuildings. It's all good. We can build a couple of shelters in that huge back area with no problem. If we could borrow Itsy and Bitsy, they could clear up all that brush behind the fence line. It's completely flat back there. You just can't see it. You can bring Licorice, and I'll get Jackson up here."

"Matt, this is fantastic!"

"There's plenty of room to put in a ring, and if you want, we can slowly build that rehab place you've always wanted. Just a few horses at a time though," he said firmly. "It'll be a lotta work."

"I can't believe it! This is perfect! I can haul down to Patrick's when I need to, and there are a ton of trails around here."

"Yep, and it'll be a real easy transition for mom and dad. Any furniture they can't fit in here, can stay exactly where it is. We can decorate over time."

"When will this happen?"

"Mom had to set them up in the downstairs guest room because she's not happy with dad goin' up and down the stairs, and she says the bathroom is too small. This house is all on one level, so it's ideal for him, and she's ready to move."

"Wow. This is so exciting."

"Puttin' up a couple of shelters out back won't take any time, and the garden shed will be just fine for a feed room 'til we can build something bigger. Mom and dad will be movin' in here over the next couple of weeks."

"This is amazing," she said softly. We'll all be together. Licorice and Jackson, you and me and Jinxy."

"That's the plan!"

Though half-asleep on his rug, when Jinx heard his name he suddenly leapt on the bed and planted his slobbery kisses over them both.

"The next order of business," Matt exclaimed, trying to push him away, "is teaching this dog to keep off this bed!"

"Don't you dare!" Dusty said, laughing out loud. "Besides, his hero status is going to last a lot longer than just a week or two."

"Right now, he needs to go," Matt said, ordering him back to his big cushion.

Though barking a protest, the border collie finally jumped to the floor and settled into his special place.

"Thank the Lord," Matt muttered. "Dusty, there's somethin' I've been wantin' to ask you. Now seems as good a time as any."

"What is it?"

"Your name. You said it was about your racin', eat my dust, but I've always had the feelin' there was somethin' else."

Her smile died away, and a slight frown crossed her brow.

"I've never told anyone," she said quietly.

"Do you wanna tell me? You don't have to."

"Yes, I think I can now," she murmured. "Around the same time you saw me with that biker in the cafe, I was totally into the sixties. Back then I felt so, uh, ugly," she said haltingly. "There was a singer, her name was Dusty Springfield, and I absolutely loved her. When my braces finally came off and I didn't have to wear those horrible glasses anymore, I thought taking her name would help me feel better. The, eat my dust thing, that was the excuse, but calling myself Dusty was all about wanting to feel beautiful—like her," she murmured, a stray tear spilling down her face, "because I never did."

"Hey," he said softly, hugging her tightly, "the most beautiful part of you isn't your long blond hair, or your face, or your body, it's your heart, and you've always had that. It was your heart that rescued Licorice and took care of him. I'll bet a lotta people saw him wastin' away in that paddock, but you jumped in with both feet. Dusty, I've dated many beautiful girls, but you're the most beautiful of them all, and not because you're a total knockout, which you are, but because of your heart."

"Matt..." she mumbled, dissolving into tears as her years of insecurity streamed out of her, "I didn't know what happiness was until, uh, you."

"You wanna know something?" he whispered, swallowing back his own rising emotion. "I swear this is the truth—neither did I."

EPILOGUE

One Year Later

DUSTY TOOK A LONG, deep breath. Licorice couldn't keep still, and she knew she wasn't helping.

Adrenalin pumped through her veins.

Every nerve in her body sparked.

One more competitor.

Then it was her turn to fly around the barrels at breakneck speed.

She wanted to win.

With a passion.

This could be her last competition.

It probably would be at this level.

She wanted to end on top.

She didn't doubt her horse. Licorice had been incredible in the months leading up to the nationals. He should win. Easily. If anything went wrong it would be down to her.

They called the next competitor.

A fresh surge of nerves rippled through her body.

Licorice began to jig.

"Easy, boy. Almost our turn. Easy now."

She glanced across at Matt standing near the in gate. As if feeling her gaze, he turned and looked back at her. Raising his hand with a thumbs up, he flashed her a wide smile. She could hear his unspoken words.

You've got this.

"Just do your thing, big boy," she murmured, stroking Licorice's neck. "I promise I won't interfere."

Sending her eyes up to the stands, she saw her cheering section. Her parents, her brother, and her aunt were all there, and so was John Draper. They'd become good friends since that dramatic day at her parents house. She wanted to win for them too.

Her name was called.

Her eyes darted to the gate. Before she even asked him to move into position, Licorice pranced forward.

"Here we go," she whispered, settling in the saddle. "Give it you're all."

She clucked.

Licorice bolted into the ring, zooming around the barrels with precision and speed beyond anything she'd ever felt from him. As he galloped back to the gate she knew their time would be off the charts. The National Championship would be theirs. Barely hearing the hooting and hollering as they slid to a sharp stop, she leaned forward and threw her arms around his neck.

"You're the best horse ever," she panted. "The absolute best." "Hey, girl, that was phenomenal," Matt exclaimed, quickly appearing at her side.

Striding up, Patrick took the reins, and sliding from the saddle, she fell into Matt's arms.

"It doesn't get better than that, Dusty," Patrick said proudly. "You've won this thing."

"It was all Licorice," she exclaimed, tears in her eyes. "I just sat there."

"Uh, you did a whole lot more than just sit there," Patrick declared, loosening the cinch. "You're a helluva rider, Dusty."

Matt chuckled.

"What he said!"

"Only four more to go," Dusty said, still leaning against Matt's chest as they moved away from the gate.

"No-one will catch you. Not a chance. I'm gonna call my folks and let them know how great you did."

"Can we wait until the class is done? I don't want to jinx anything."

"Sure, and speakin' of Jinx, I hope he hasn't been causin' them too much trouble."

"Jinx? Never. He's perfect."

"Like you," he murmured, quickly kissing her.

DUSTY'S TIME HELD, and as she rode into the ring to collect the gold trophy, she barely managed to fight back the threatening wave of emotion. The officials were all there, the ribbon was placed around her horse's neck, and she was handed the gleaming prize, but as the applause died down Matt jogged into the ring. He had no business being there, but when Dusty glanced at the show manager he didn't seem surprised, and handed Matt the microphone.

"Hey everyone. My name's Matt Montgomery," he began. "I've know Dusty Anderson since she was just a kid."

The crowd fell silent.

"Matt," she whispered, "what are you doing?"

"She just asked me what I'm doin'?" he continued, "and I'm sure ya'll are wonderin' too. Dusty, would you mind gettin' off that handsome horse for a minute?"

Completely confounded, she handed the trophy to the nearest official and climbed from the saddle.

"Thank you, darlin'," he murmured, then to her shock, still holding the microphone, he dropped to one knee. "Dusty, I love you with all my heart, and you'd make me the happiest man on God's green earth if you'd agree to be my wife."

"Oh, my gosh...yes...of course..."

The audience erupted.

Rising to his feet and handing the microphone to the official, he withdrew a black velvet box from his jeans pocket. With the crowd still cheering, he slipped the diamond ring on Dusty's finger. She stared at it for a moment, then looked up at him with wide eyes.

"It's pink. You've given me a pink diamond."

DUSTY'S FATHER HAD been made manager of the new depot, and his salary had doubled. With Licorice gone, her parents no longer needed the acreage and sold the house, upgrading to a brand new home in an upscale development. Dusty had been sad to see the homestead go, but had found comfort walking through the gleaming new home, and seeing the happiness shine from her mother's eyes.

"Life's a bit like a trail ride. You never know what's around the next corner," her mother had said. "There's nothing so constant as change."

As she sat at the dinner table in the hotel restaurant with John, Patrick, Sharon, her brother and her parents, celebrating her win and the engagement, her mother's wise words rang through her head.

"Hey, darlin', are you okay?" Matt asked quietly.

"I've never been better."

"You're sure?"

"I'm very sure, though you're right, there is something I need to tell you, but not here."

He seemed satisfied, and she threw herself back into the happy conversation. When the dinner broke up, Matt hurried her into the elevator, then down the hall to their hotel room.

"So, what's goin' on?" he asked, the moment they walked through the door.

"Today was...," but her voice trailed off as tears spilled down her cheeks.

"Dusty! Darlin', what's wrong," he asked urgently, wrapping her in his arms. "Tell me what's upset you like this?"

"Nothing, I'm really, really happy."

"So why the tears?"

"I'm just—today was the last day I'll be competing, at least for a while."

"Is that why you're upset."

"I'm not upset. Sorry. The thing is, Matt...oh, lord...you're going to be a daddy."

"Say, what?" he breathed, pulling back and staring at her.

"Is that okay?"

"Okay? Okay? Are you kiddin' me?" he exclaimed, sweeping her up and spinning her around. "That's the best news I've ever had in my life! How long have you known?"

"Put me down and I'll tell you."

"Tell me and I'll put you down."

"Only about a week, but I didn't say anything because—"

"Because you were afraid I'd be worried and not let you compete," he declared, setting her on her feet.

"Something like that."

"But your doc said it was okay?"

"As long as I didn't fall off."

He looked at her in horror.

"I'm kidding!"

"You're lucky I'm too excited to spank you," he said with a chuckle.

"But that won't stop you later."

"Oh, no darlin', but right now I just wanna lie down and hold you," he said, taking her hand and leading her to the bed. "I can't wait to go pony shoppin'," he muttered as they stretched out and she snuggled against him. "Maybe I'll start a line of tiny saddles for little ones. Dang! A baby! Dang! I've gotta rope my brain around this."

"Matt," she whispered, lifting her head to look at him, "will you promise me something?"

"Anything. Tell me and it's done."

"Mom said life's like a trail ride. You never know what's around the corner."

"Huh. I guess that's true."

"Will you promise to stay on the trail with me, no matter what?"

"You wouldn't be wearing that pretty pink ring if I wasn't prepared to do that," he said solemnly, then breaking into a grin, he added, "and as long as you've got those hot pink chaps I won't be goin' anywhere!"

THE END

DEAR Reader:

Thank you for buying this book. If you have a moment I would greatly appreciate your review. I constantly strive to bring you interesting and enjoyable content and your feedback is valued. Feel free to contact me at any time. I love to hear from readers. My email is: MagCarpenter@yahoo.com, and here are my social media links should you care to check them out.

My very best wishes,

Maggie

BOOKS BY MAGGIE CARPENTER

ROUGH COWBOY
HUNKS and HORSES
Four Book Series/HEA-StandaloneC
Featuring characters from
COWBOY: His Ranch. His Rules. His Secrets
TO KISS A COWBOY.
TO CATCH A COWBOY.
TO CON A COWBOY.
TO TRUST A COWBOY:
SEXY SCIFI - PARANORMAL
ROUGH ALPHA
TRAINED BY THE ALIEN:
WARLOCK :
THE ALIEN'S RULES:
BDSM CONTEMPORARY ROMANCE
WET 1
WET 2
SINS BEHIND THE SCENES:
I AM A DOMINANT:
DESIRE UNLEASHED - Sexsomnia.
TIMELESS OBSESSION:
For a full list of her novels visit her author page.
https://www.amazon.com/author/maggiecarpenter
http://www.MaggieCarpenter.com
https://www.facebook.com/MaggieCarpenterWriter

www.ingramcontent.com/pod-product-compliance
Lightning Source LLC
Chambersburg PA
CBHW050935120626
46552CB00001B/220